GUIDING GEMMA:

An Age Gap Cowboy Daddy Romance

SUE LYNDON

CHAPTER 1

GEMMA

I T WAS PERFECT. N EWLY RENOVATED, THE INTERIOR of the red brick building featured hardwood floors, picture frame wall molding in every room, and a massive bay window that overlooked the picturesque town of Rocky Springs. The outside was equally stunning with freshly painted white shutters, a huge front porch with an old-fashioned glider, and a well-tended garden in the back.

Home, sweet, home? Dare I dream?

The best part, the most important part, was that the bottom level of the house had once served as a meeting hall. Which meant plenty of room for my art studio.

And the upper level... well, it was a dream. It contained a studio apartment complete with a cottage-style kitchen, a master bathroom with a clawfoot tub *and* a standup shower, and other adorable details that made me one hundred percent sure this was the house for me.

"As you can see, Ms. Wilder," Sarah, the rental agent, said in a gushing tone, "I believe this building would work well for the business you described. Not only is it immaculate and move-in ready, but the zoning is for both commercial and residential. Plus, this street gets lots of foot traffic from tourists." She opened her arms and spun in a slow circle. "I can easily picture this place as an art studio."

"Well, the rent is more than reasonable," I said, and I couldn't help but smile. For the first time in forever, I felt hopeful. "And you're right, the building *is* immaculate." Knowing I could move in right away was also a big plus. The movers were arriving in Rocky Springs later today with the first batch of my belongings. While the current plan was for them to meet me at a storage facility, I could easily call and inform them of the change of plans.

"So, what do you say? Are you ready to sign the lease?"

I turned to face Sarah, took a deep breath, and nodded. "Yes, I'm ready. I'll take it." Excitement swept through me, and a weight was lifted off my shoulders. I'd only been in Rocky Springs for a few hours, but already I believed that maybe, just maybe, I could make a fresh start here. A new beginning far from my hometown in Connecticut, far from the painful scandal that had caused me to run away from the only life I'd ever known.

"Excellent. Let's head back to my office and we'll work out all the details. As I said, the place is move-in ready, so once the papers are signed, you can consider it yours. Sleep here tonight if you want. I think you'll like it here, and I daresay you'll like your landlord too." The rental agent's gaze turned wistful, and she placed a hand dramatically over her heart. "Derek Bolt. He owns Rocky Springs Ranch and Resort, as well as a good number of buildings in town. I promise he's an attentive landlord. If you ever need anything fixed, he'll be quick to help you and most of the time he does the repairs personally. Oh, and he's also very, very easy on the eyes." She fished something out of her pocket and handed it to me.

"Oh?" My breath caught in my throat as I stared at the landlord/rancher's business card. In his late forties (I guessed) and ruggedly handsome, he stood in front of a bale of hay wearing a snug flannel shirt and a black cowboy hat. My pulse fluttered.

"My niece is a photographer and took this photo," Sarah said. "She freelances in photography, but she also writes articles for the Rocky Springs Daily. Tell you what, I'll put in a good word, and I bet she'll do a write-up about your new business. You know, once you get things up and running." Sarah regarded me with a look of warmth that took me aback, and I found myself blinking away tears.

I turned and pretended to gaze out the window as I fought to regain control of my emotions. I wasn't used to people being nice to me. I was used to snide comments, gossipy whispers, and looks of pity. Looks of disgust, too. Those were the worst. It had been so long since anyone had treated me like a real person that I was having difficulty processing it.

Finally, I managed to calm myself enough to turn around. "Thank you, Sarah. I would love to talk to your niece once I get this place up and running. That's very kind of you to offer." I cast another look out the bay window, my eyes drawn to the snow-capped mountains in the distance. A sense of freedom stole through me, and my resolve to build a life here in Rocky Springs hardened. I could do it. I could make it. And the asshole back east who'd tried to ruin my life could suck a bag of dicks.

"Oh, I'm happy to help," Sarah said with a sigh. "Let's head back to my office and we'll get those papers signed. I'll text my assistant and have him pick up some sandwiches for us from Kay's Diner. Do you like BLT's? Or how about chicken salad?"

"A BLT sounds great. Thank you." I swallowed past the burning in my throat. Sarah's continued kindness had me on the verge of crying. I breathed a sigh of relief when she turned to exit the house, and I took a moment to wipe a tear away in secret.

Once I stepped onto the porch, I breathed deeply of the fresh mountain air. *Home*, I told myself. *This town is my new home.*

It's my fresh start.

A place where I (hopefully) won't have to hide any longer.

CHAPTER 2

DEREK

Sadness clutched me as I stared at the words etched into the gravestone.

Trisha Bolt, Beloved Wife and Daughter.

Five years. She'd been gone five years and sometimes it felt like yesterday. Other times it felt like a hundred years or more. It had been too long since I'd held her in my arms and told her I loved her, too long since we laughed together or took a starlit walk on the ranch.

When I blinked, a vision of the accident scene flashed in my mind. A little blue car smashed underneath a tractor trailer. The rescue crew trying desperately to get the passenger out of the car, even though it was obvious that anyone inside couldn't have survived.

I remembered the sheriff holding me back while

the first responders finally pulled her body from the mangled car. I remembered the hoarseness of my throat as I screamed and cried and cursed God.

Lastly, I remembered her bloodied body and the limpness of her hand after I managed to fight the sheriff off and rush to her side.

I gave my head a harsh shake and knelt to place a bouquet of wildflowers atop the gravestone. Trisha's favorite. She used to walk in the meadow near our home in the mornings, and during the springtime or early summer, she would always come back with wild-flowers.

"I miss you," I whispered, still kneeling before the gravestone. I placed a hand upon the cool surface and bowed my head. "I hope you're resting easy, love." My throat closed up and I couldn't utter another word.

I wasn't sure how long I stayed like that, silently speaking to Trisha. When my legs were almost numb from the kneeling position, I rose to my feet and wiped away a few tears.

The phone in my pocket kept vibrating, but I ignored it. Business could wait. My Sunday morning visits to Trisha were more important. And since today was also the five-year anniversary of her death, I felt like I ought to stay for a while longer.

So, I did. I stood in front of her grave with my head bowed, wishing I could turn back the clock five years and a day.

Eventually, a cloud cover rolled in, and the breeze picked up. As a soft rain began to fall, I finally headed to my truck.

Time to go home.

Time to face another night alone.

THE NEXT DAY

I PARKED IN FRONT OF THE LARGE BRICK BUILDING on Main Street, then grabbed my tool bag and other supplies from the back of the truck. Nothing gave me purpose like fixing up the rental properties I owned in Rocky Springs. Having grown up in poverty, I knew what it was like to have shitty landlords. Now that I was a landlord myself, I was determined to be a good one.

Standing on the sidewalk in front of the house, I glanced around to make sure the exterior was perfect. Just last week, I'd replaced a few bricks and painted the shutters. After a recent remodel, the inside was nearly complete and ready for the next tenant, I just needed to add the final trim to the kitchen cabinets. I'd already informed my rental agent, Sarah, that she could start showing the house, though to my knowledge, no one had shown any interest yet.

I unlocked the door and strode inside, heading straight for the stairs. Like many of the buildings I owned in town, this one contained space for a store (most likely, another gift shop that would cater to tourists) and a spacious apartment on the second floor.

Ever since I'd started buying up and remodeling houses and buildings on Main Street years ago, business in Rocky Springs had exploded. This was great for the town and for me personally, as it meant more wealthy tourists came for the "ranch experience" at Rocky Springs Ranch and Resort.

When I was a kid growing up in this town, we never had tourists. Not unless they had no choice but to stop here for gas. Rocky Springs used to be a rundown town nobody cared to visit. I was proud to have done my part to help turn it around. Proud to call this beautiful town home. I loved the people here. In Rocky Springs, everyone looked out for their neighbor.

I froze once I reached the upstairs apartment. Hm. There were boxes strewn about the floor. Looked like someone was in the process of moving in. But how could that be?

Shit. I hadn't answered my phone yesterday, nor had I finished checking all my messages. It was possible I had a message waiting from Sarah about a new tenant.

"Hello?" I called out, feeling like an intruder. "Anybody home?"

I stared at the closed bedroom door. Had I shut it last time I was here? I couldn't remember.

"Hello?" I called out again. "Hellooooo?"

CHAPTER 3

GEMMA

I awoke with a start, then relaxed once I realized where I was. Rocky Springs. In my new house. A rental, but it still felt like mine.

As I yawned widely, I stretched under the covers. I reached for my favorite stuffie, Mr. Rabbit, and hugged him tightly to my chest. Satisfaction filled me as I gazed around my room.

I'd worked late into the night unpacking and getting it set up just the way I wanted. I'd hung fairy lights and put up my favorite wall art, mostly abstract paintings of baby animals I'd created myself. The bed was filled with fancy pink, lace-trimmed pillows, and matching sheets with a warm comforter. About a dozen stuffies were piled into the corner of the bed against the wall, but I had a few more boxes of them I needed to unpack.

Stacks of books were scattered throughout my bedroom and there were two large piles on the nightstand too. I hoped that sometime this week, perhaps even today, I could purchase some bookshelves. I would have to wait until the movers arrived with the rest of my belongings, however, since they were due to show up around noon today. Yesterday, a truck had brought my personal belongings, but today my paintings and other supplies for my art studio would arrive.

I couldn't wait to set up shop, and I began compiling a mental list of all the tasks that awaited me.

"Hello? Anybody home?"

I clutched the covers and gasped at the sound of a deep, masculine voice that had come from the other side of my bedroom door. A robber? A serial killer? A murderous clown? My imagination ran wild.

"Hello? Helloooo?"

There it was again. The voice sounded friendly enough, but it still made me uneasy that someone had just walked into my new home. My stomach flipped when I remembered that I had absolutely locked the front door last night. Back door, too, and I'd even checked the downstairs windows.

Well. Whoever it was had broken in.

With shaking hands, I grabbed my cell phone off the nightstand and dialed 9-1-1.

Except, the call didn't go through.

No signal. Wonderful.

I'd managed to make a few calls last night, though reception had been spotty. I got out of bed quietly and held the phone up, trying in desperation to get a signal.

A sudden knock on my bedroom door caused me to gasp and drop my phone. It hit the floor with an audible clatter. My heart raced and my palms became sweaty. Well, if the intruder didn't already know I was here, they knew now.

I glanced around my room, looking for something I could use as a weapon, but came up woefully empty. Best I could do would be to throw a shoe, a stuffie, or a book at their head.

"Good morning! Sounds like there's someone in there. Sorry to bother you. Also, my apologies for just walking right in. Hope I didn't give you a scare. Didn't realize the place had been rented out already. Name's Derek Bolt and I'm your landlord. I'm here to put the final trim on the kitchen cabinets, but if now's a bad time, I can come back later." The voice was close, directly on the other side of my door.

Derek Bolt. My landlord.

I glanced at the business card that rested on the nightstand and breathed a sigh of relief. Of course. The big-time rancher who also happened to own a whole bunch of buildings in Rocky Springs. Sarah had continued gushing about him as I signed papers yesterday, and she hadn't had a bad thing to say.

I took a few deep breaths in an effort to calm myself.

No big deal. Just my super sexy landlord.

Not a murderous clown.

What a relief. Sort of.

I smoothed my hair into place, took another deep breath, and opened the bedroom door. My eyes instantly met with a gorgeous deep blue gaze. I swallowed past the sudden dryness in my throat as I took in the details of the oh-so-handsome man standing before me.

Broad shoulders. Dimples. A hint of dark hair peeking out from his cowboy hat. An unshaven jaw that made my fingers tingle to stroke his face. He also towered over my five-foot-five frame by about a foot.

While the picture of Derek Bolt on the business card was nice, it didn't do the man justice. In person, he looked like a sexy Hollywood actor who'd just walked off the set of a cowboy movie. My tummy fluttered as I took in the sight of his form-fitting jeans and his large belt buckle that was polished to a gleam.

"Um, hello, Mr. Bolt," I found myself saying as I forced my gaze back to his eyes. I noticed he was taking stock of me too and couldn't help but flush. What did he think of me?

"Good morning, ma'am." He placed his tool bag and other supplies on the floor. He tipped his hat at me, and I nearly swooned on the spot.

But then I glanced down at myself and cringed. Oh no. No no no. I was wearing ladybug-print, drop-seat footie pajamas. And I was also still clutching Mr. Rabbit. Yeah, I'd dropped my phone but not my stuffie.

Shameful memories flooded me, and I backed up a few steps, suddenly dizzy. I grasped onto the doorway for support.

"Hey there, darlin', let's get you off your feet. You don't look so good." He guided me back to my bed and helped me sit down. "You all right?" His calm, steady voice washed over me.

My face had never felt so hot as I stared up into his concerned gaze. His kind eyes. If he thought a twenty-five-year-old wearing footie pajamas and carrying a stuffie around was weird, it didn't show on his face.

"I'm fine, thank you," I finally managed to say. "Just stood up too fast and got a little dizzy, that's all." I hoped he believed my lie. How could I tell the truth? Especially to a stranger? Compassionate or not, he would probably think I was strange. I was tired of people thinking I was strange. I wanted to be normal in Rocky Springs, though in my defense, I never thought anyone would see me in my footie pajamas or glimpse the inside of my ultra-girly bedroom.

With a gentle touch, he placed a finger beneath my chin, tipping my face upward. "Are you sure you're okay, darlin'? I could have Dr. Humphrey here within minutes."

"Oh, really, I'm fine. No need for a doctor."

His nearness and his touch, as well as the scent of his cologne, rich and woodsy, yet subtle and masculine, caused little tremors of warmth to surge to my core. I found myself squeezing my legs together and squirming in place, pleasantly unsettled by the blissful ache that stirred in my nether region.

The caring glint in Derek Bolt's eyes only increased my attraction to him.

And while he was a stranger, I didn't feel unsafe in his presence.

Far from it.

Daddy vibes. He gave off daddy vibes.

Protective, cuddly daddy vibes.

This realization made my face heat further. I swallowed hard and tried to look away, but he grasped my chin between two fingers and lifted his other hand in front of my face. He held up one finger and moved it from left to right in the air.

"Follow my finger, please."

I obeyed, though I felt incredibly silly. Of all the ways to meet the handsome rancher from the business card I'd spent way too much time staring at last night...

Of course it would be like this.

Caught off guard. In my footie pajamas.

While I was having one of my nervous dizzy spells.

I regretted not rising earlier and putting on some real clothes. Some grown-up clothes.

Did he think I was ridiculous for being dressed like this? Did he find me childish?

I reminded myself of his gentle yet authoritative demeanor. And the fact that I could easily imagine him as a daddy to my little girl.

Maybe he wouldn't judge me.

What if he really was a daddy dom?

Dare I hope?

CHAPTER 4

DEREK

I STEPPED AWAY FROM THE YOUNG WOMAN, satisfied that she wasn't about to pass out. She looked far more alert than she had a few seconds ago, and she'd followed my finger without any difficulty.

I offered her my hand. "Again, sorry to surprise you this morning. Derek Bolt." Had I already told her my name? I couldn't remember. The adorable woman had me so flustered I couldn't think straight. Not only was she beautiful and far too innocent looking, but I also suspected she might be a little.

Her attire, as well as the numerous stuffies on her bed, plus the daddy dom romance books stacked on the nightstand gave her away. A few titles caught my eye in particular: *Who's Your Daddy*, *Tamed by Daddy*, *A Little in Trouble*, and *Claiming His Little Girl*.

I refocused my attention on the young woman

whose name I didn't yet know. After a moment's hesitation, she shyly reached out and accepted my hand.

A jolt of sensation passed between us as we shook hands, and my pants started to feel too tight.

"It's nice to meet you, Mr. Bolt. I'm Gemma Wilder. I, um, I just signed the lease papers yesterday afternoon and already started moving in. I hope that's okay. If I'm not supposed to be here yet…" Her voice trailed off and her dark eyes filled with sadness.

"Gemma. That's a pretty name and it suits you." I dropped her hand and stepped back. "And you are totally fine moving in already. Sounds like this is your new home. Oh, and you can call me Daddy."

What? I felt my eyes widen.

Had I really just said that?

"Derek," I blurted a bit louder than necessary as I corrected my blunder. "You can call me Derek. Instead of Mr. Bolt. *Derek.*"

Her mouth fell open and she looked at me in shock. Her cheeks promptly grew pink, and she drew in a quick breath. "Right. Derek. It's nice to meet you." She cast a brief glance at the books, no doubt realizing I'd glimpsed a few of the titles.

I flashed her a smile, hoping to alleviate the sudden tension between us. "Well, I would say I've done a fine job of making our first meeting awkward."

Her abrupt laughter was like a balm to my soul. She grinned up at me, and I was relieved to see she no longer appeared worried or surprised or uneasy. Good. I wanted her to feel completely safe in my presence.

Wait. Where had that thought come from?

"Oh? You mean when you broke in while I was sleeping and then told me to call you 'Daddy?' What's awkward about that?" she said in a playful tone. Her dark eyes twinkled brighter.

Now it was my turn to laugh, and God how the sensation felt strange. But also good. I didn't laugh often. Didn't smile often either. But the laughter rumbled from my chest, and I even felt it in my stomach.

Lower, I experienced something else entirely.

All at once, my jeans became even tighter. Constricting.

Before I could turn to pick up my tool bag, I noticed Gemma's gaze had drifted to my crotch.

I also noticed she flushed a deeper shade of pink.

Jesus. I needed to get a grip.

I spun on my heel and grabbed my tool bag and the pieces of trim. "Sorry I bothered you, Gemma. I'll come back later."

"Wait! You can stay. You can install the trim now. It won't bother me." There was a hopefulness in her voice that I couldn't ignore, and I didn't want to see her looking sad again, so I turned around to face her while holding the tool bag in front of my crotch.

"Are you certain you don't mind?" I wanted to be sure. I didn't want to scare her. She was a woman alone in a house with a man she'd just met. Landlord or not, she would have every right to want me gone.

"I'm certain." She offered me a sweet, reassuring smile that made me want to scoop her up in my arms and press a kiss to her forehead.

The affectionate and protective urges she was drawing from me left me so stunned, I forgot to breathe for a few seconds.

"Well, then, I'd better get to work," I said after I recovered from the shock. I fled her bedroom and hurried to the kitchen, my heart pounding nearly as fast as my dick. I was rock hard and a bit breathless.

I didn't feel like myself at all. Flustered. For the first time in forever, I'd gotten flustered in front of a woman.

Also, for the first time in forever, I'd *looked* at a woman. Actually looked at a woman and desired her. Ached for her.

Guilt visited me a moment later, and my excitement started fading.

Since Trisha's passing, I'd never thought I would experience an attraction to another woman again. My reaction to Gemma had shaken me to my very core. With an unsteady hand, I gathered the tiny nails I needed to secure the trim to the bottom of the cabinets.

As I worked, I heard soft footfalls behind me. I peeked over my shoulder and nearly dropped the hammer. Gemma was standing in the middle of the kitchen wearing a light pink dress that hugged her bosom but flared outward. Ruffles adorned the hem and the sleeves of the dress, and she wore a pair of matching pink sandals. Her sleek golden waves were secured with a white headband that had tiny pink flowers on it.

Adorable.

Not for the first time in her presence, I forgot how to breathe as I stared at her.

Yes, she was most definitely a little.

You can call me Daddy.

I still couldn't believe I'd said that.

"I would offer you some coffee or something to drink," she said with a glance around the kitchen, "but I'm afraid I haven't been grocery shopping yet." Her stomach promptly rumbled, and she flushed as she tucked an errant strand of hair behind her ear.

I hurried to place the final touches on the trim, then jumped to my feet. All the other work I had waiting for me today vanished from my mind. The only thing that mattered was Gemma's comfort and well-being. The little girl was hungry, and I wanted to see her fed. I also wanted to make sure she got groceries in the house soon. The desire to take care of her needs was so strong I couldn't ignore it.

"Actually, Gemma, I'd like to take you out for breakfast. Kay's Diner? It's a short drive from here and they have the best pancakes in the world." I held my breath as I awaited her response.

Her face brightened. "Well, I don't normally go to breakfast with complete strangers who break into my house," she said in a teasing voice, "but you look really cute in that cowboy hat, so sure, why not? Plus, I really love pancakes."

CHAPTER 5

GEMMA

I WAS OPENLY FLIRTING WITH THE HANDSOME rancher and we both knew it. I felt reckless but also free.

I reminded myself that I could be whoever I wanted to be in this town, but I would always be a little at heart, no matter how grown-up I tried to present myself on the outside.

Would Derek like the real me? Did he realize I was a little?

I was ninety-eight percent certain he was a daddy, and not just because of his earlier slip of tongue. *You can call me Daddy.* I flushed at the memory.

A look of relief had entered Derek's eyes once I accepted his invitation, and a smile had also tugged at his lips. Lips I kept staring at and thinking about kissing. When I wasn't trying to get a glimpse of the bulge in his pants, that was.

"You think I'm cute?" he asked, and his dimples became more pronounced. His eyes twinkled with amusement. "*Cute?*"

I flushed. Was it getting hot in here?

"Well, you're certainly easy on the eyes," I said, borrowing a line from Sarah. Fortunately, it was the right thing to say, because it earned me another chuckle from him. "Let me grab my purse and we can head out."

I rushed back to my bedroom, feeling on top of the world. I had a breakfast date! With the oh-so-sexy cowboy daddy who also happened to be my landlord.

Also happened to be at least twenty years older than me.

What could go wrong?

A moment of panic rose as I started to imagine all the things that *could* go wrong. What if I'd misread him completely? Or what if he learned about my reasons for fleeing Connecticut? Would he judge me? Look at me with disgust?

I grabbed my purse and took a few deep breaths.

You've got this. It's just breakfast. It doesn't have to go any further than pancakes and coffee.

You are strong and you are brave. You moved across the country all by yourself and you're about to open a freaking business in a brand-new town. You're a rockstar.

Trying to ignore my nerves, I retrieved my phone from the floor, shoved it into my purse, and departed the bedroom with a spring in my step and hope in my heart.

❧❦❧

I STARED AT THE MENU IN AWE. KAY'S DINER HAD *ten* different kinds of pancakes. Plain. Strawberry. Chocolate Chip. Blueberry. Rainbow Sprinkles. And so on. I gnawed on my bottom lip as I tried to reach a decision.

"Well?" came the cowboy's deep voice from across the table. "Know what you want yet?"

My pulse jumped when I looked up from the menu and met his gorgeous blue eyes. Had I ever met anyone with eyes so blue before? I didn't think so. And those dimples. Every time he smiled, I found myself squirming in my seat as the heated pulses between my thighs built and built.

"Um," I glanced back at the menu. "I think I'll go with Rainbow Sprinkle Pancakes with a fruit cup on the side. And coffee."

He lifted one dark eyebrow at me. "Coffee? Are you sure? That's a very grown-up drink, Gemma, don't you think?" There was a knowing gleam in his stare when my head shot up and I peered at him in shock.

He was calling me out as a little. He was letting me know that *he knew my secret*. But there was an understanding look in his eyes too, and a spark of excitement on top of that.

I flushed when his leg touched mine under the table and he didn't move it away. "Uh, if I don't drink at least two cups of coffee every morning, I'm not a very pleasant person. Trust me, you don't want to see me caffeine deprived and grumpy."

"Hm." He stroked his chin for a moment. "Well, I suppose you'd better get the coffee then. Grumpy little girls have a tendency to get in trouble, and we wouldn't want that to happen, would we?" He leaned forward and spoke in a deep but hushed voice so no one around us might overhear.

A pang of heat surged to my feminine core.

Holy crap on a whole wheat cracker, this guy was for real a daddy.

And he was absolutely one hundred and fifty percent flirting with me.

My spirits soared and excitement coursed through me, causing a full body flush. I was starting to feel feverish in his presence, and a bit tongue tied. I still hadn't responded to his statement about little girls getting into trouble. I tried to think of something witty but came up empty.

"Well, I try to be a good girl," I finally whispered, "but sometimes I can't help being naughty. It just happens." There wasn't enough oxygen in the room. My breaths became shallow and faint and there was a strange buzzing in my head. This couldn't really be happening, could it?

A stern yet playful look came over Derek aka *You can call me Daddy*. Butterflies swarmed in my tummy, and I couldn't stop fidgeting in my seat. The ache between my thighs was getting worse.

"Well, it sounds like you need a daddy to keep you

in line, little girl," he said, not blinking as he held my gaze.

"I-I've never actually had a daddy before," I admitted shyly. I could hardly believe I was opening up to him and so quickly. But it felt right, and I couldn't seem to stop myself. "My last boyfriend thought I was weird when I told him what I wanted. He said I was disgusting." Tears burned in my eyes, and I lowered my head, allowing my hair to obscure my face to hide my stricken expression.

He reached across the table and grasped my hand in his. He gave it a gentle squeeze. "Hey, look at me, baby girl. Gemma, look at me."

Finally, I lifted my gaze and met his eyes. Eyes that still shone with compassion.

"Listen to me, sweet girl. You're not disgusting. I'm sorry you had a boyfriend who treated you badly and didn't understand your needs. It sounds like you might be new to the lifestyle and—" He stopped speaking when the waitress approached to take our order. I felt bereft when he released my hand.

I blinked fast and hoped it didn't look like I'd been crying. No tears had fallen, but I felt incredibly fragile right then. If someone were too kind to me or said the wrong thing, I very well might break down into tears. Time for another pep talk.

I'm brave. I'm brave. I'm not disgusting or weird or...

"Good morning, Kay," Derek said with a nod at the smiling middle-aged woman who'd come to take our order.

"Mornin', Derek. It's good to see you. How have

you been?" She flashed a curious smile my way. "And good mornin' to you as well, miss. Are you Derek's niece or something?" She winked at me, and I blushed hard as I went from thinking of Derek as my *daddy* to my *uncle*. Both scenarios left me breathless and aching with desire.

Derek chuckled. "Now, Kay, you know very well that I don't have any nieces or nephews."

Kay smirked, though not in a mean way. "Oh, I'm just teasing and you know that. So, is she a new friend? Or maybe a business partner? Or a hot date?" She giggled and I noticed a few nearby patrons glance our way, and I resisted the urge to sink lower in my seat and hide.

Logically, I realized she was just teasing, and given Derek's look of ease I knew this was banter between friends. Kay seemed like a nice lady, but also nosey, and the thought of anyone finding out my secrets left me deeply unsettled. Thankfully, Derek's response helped to relax me.

"Kay, meet Gemma Wilder. She just rented out the old meeting hall on Main Street. She's new in town. Or, at least I think she is. Truth is, we haven't had a chance to talk much yet, but we were both hungry, so I thought we'd come get some of your world-famous pancakes."

Kay's eyebrows shot up as she looked at me, and I swallowed quickly before answering her unspoken questions. "Yep, he's right. I'm new in town. Just moved here from Connecticut. Going to open an art studio soon."

"Oh that's wonderful!" Kay gushed. "Well, let me take your order and then you two lovebirds can get to know one another."

Derek shot her an overly annoyed glance when she said *lovebirds* that almost made me laugh. It also made me wonder what he might look like when he was in stern daddy-mode. My butt cheeks tingled as I listened to him place our order.

CHAPTER 6

DEREK

"As I was saying," I said once Kay departed our table, "it sounds like you're new to the lifestyle. How long have you been a little, Gemma?"

She shot me a shy glance, then looked at her lap as she fidgeted with her hands.

"Gemma?"

She met my gaze and flushed. God, every time she flushed, my cock got harder. It would be a miracle if I didn't bust a hole in my jeans during breakfast. I resisted the urge to readjust myself under the table, conscious of the curious glances other diners kept shooting our way. Not that I could blame them for staring. In the five years since Trisha's passing, I'd never once taken a woman out for a meal.

"I guess you could say I'm new to the lifestyle," Gemma finally replied. "I've always felt different and had certain... desires. It wasn't until I started reading daddy dom romance books that I understood what I was and why I felt different. Then I began to embrace my little side. I started dressing the way I really wanted and..." Her face turned bright red, and she swallowed hard.

"And what?" I prompted. "It's okay, Gemma. You can tell me. I won't think you're weird. I promise."

She hesitated for a moment before continuing. "Well, I like collecting stuffies and watching cartoons, and coloring in coloring books. Um, that's usually how I spend my evenings. It helps me relax and feel more like myself. Well, and also reading naughty daddy dom romance books. I usually read a book a night. It's my favorite escape." She sighed. "It took me over two years of dating my boyfriend to work up the nerve to tell him about my interest in age play, and it didn't go so well. Yet here I am telling you about it, and we only met an hour ago. It's funny how life works."

"Maybe it's fate." I could easily imagine myself as Gemma's daddy. Tending to her every need. Showering her with affection. Guiding her and encouraging her. And yes, even punishing her when she required correction.

A look of longing entered the sweet little girl's gaze, and I reached for her hand again and gave it a squeeze. Her eyes widened and her cheeks turned a pretty shade of pink. Her breath also hitched, and I noticed her squirming in her seat. A little girl squirming around in her seat meant one of two things.

"Is something wrong, little girl? Do you have to go

potty, or are you getting achy between your thighs?" I knew I'd just asked a bold question, and perhaps I was moving too fast, but I was enjoying my interactions with Gemma far too much to back down. Magic sparked between us each time our eyes met, and I couldn't help but revel in her shy, nervous expression as she considered whether to answer my question.

She drew in a deep breath and her hand trembled in mine. "It's, um, the second one," she whispered, and her admission made my cock ache something fierce.

"You're getting achy between your thighs, baby girl?"

She nodded. "Y-yes." She squirmed in her seat again, her movements a bit exaggerated as a look of mischief flitted across her face. "Very achy."

Jesus. I glanced around to make sure no one was looking, then I finally readjusted my cock in my pants. It didn't help much. The strain against the zipper almost had me groaning. I bit the inside of my cheek to keep from making any embarrassing noises in the middle of Kay's Diner. Then I refocused my attention on the mischievous little girl seated across from me. I strongly suspected she knew about my predicament and was delighting in making it worse.

But two could play at this game, and I intended to win.

"If you can't control the naughty thoughts you're having, baby girl, the thoughts that are making your privates so achy, you'll end up making a mess in your panties."

Her eyes went wide, and she gasped just as Kay returned with our coffee. We both fell silent as Kay set the drinks on the table, winked at us, and sashayed away while humming a show tune I couldn't quite place. I had no doubt the whole town would be talking about my date with Gemma by lunchtime, but I tried to tell myself it didn't matter.

So what if they talked? I wasn't doing anything wrong. Sure, a few eyebrows might raise over the age difference between us, but it's not as though anyone would have a clue that I was her daddy.

Her daddy.

I couldn't stop envisioning myself as her daddy.

I wanted to see her again. Soon.

Hell, I wanted this date to last all day. Into the night, even.

The prospect of falling asleep with sweet little Gemma nestled in my arms filled me with longing.

But no. She was new to the lifestyle. Had never really experienced it before. But she wouldn't stop flushing or squirming, and she'd already admitted that she'd grown achy between her thighs.

If I reached a hand under her skirt and ran a finger over the crotch of her panties, would I discover she'd already soaked through the undergarment?

Heated waves of desire swept over me as I imagined peeling down her panties to find a large wet spot, her nether lips gleaming pink with her arousal.

She poured a small amount of cream into her coffee, added two packets of sugar, and stirred. But when she lifted the spoon from her cup, she held my gaze as she suggestively licked it.

I gave her my sternest look. "Might I remind you that we're in public? In a family restaurant, no less. If you were *my* baby girl, Gemma, I would march you out to the truck and smack your bottom a few times." I plucked the spoon from her hand. "I'm confiscating this since you can't behave yourself, young lady."

She gave me a sassy look that made my palm twitch, but before either of us could speak, Kay bustled over with our pancakes.

"Here you go, folks. And just in time, it would seem. You both look famished."

CHAPTER 7

GEMMA

I couldn't stop replaying Derek's words.

If you were my baby girl, Gemma, I would march you out to the truck and smack your bottom a few times.

I snuck a peek at his large hands. Oh yeah. I bet he could really spank a bottom with those big sexy daddy hands. A thrill rushed through me, and a fresh ache pulsed in my nether region.

We ate our pancakes in silence, though our eyes kept meeting. And every time we looked at one another, my pulse spiked, and I had trouble breathing.

Eventually, the diner cleared out. Only two patrons remained, an elderly couple who were seated in the far corner of the restaurant. Kay refilled our coffee cups and then disappeared into the back, and the other servers weren't anywhere to be seen either.

Taking advantage of our solitude, I added more

cream and sugar to my coffee before boldly snatching my stolen spoon back. I stirred the coffee and then made an elaborate show of defiling the utensil with my tongue. All this as Derek watched with an increasingly stern glint in those sexy blue eyes of his.

"That's twice now. If you were my baby girl," he said in an ominous tone that made my tummy flutter, "you'd get a quick spanking in the truck and then another one—a much longer, harder one—once we got home. Suffice it to say, you'd end up with a very sore, very red little bottom by the time I was finished meting out your punishment."

"Is that so?" *Daddy*. I really wanted to call him Daddy, but it didn't quite feel so bold yet. Sure, he kept calling me little girl and baby girl, but that was different. At least I thought it was. Calling him Daddy seemed more intimate, and I didn't want to use the title without a firm invitation.

"Yes, that's so," he said in a scolding tone. "Now straighten up, young lady. Behave yourself. Don't make me tell you again."

I twirled the spoon from hand to hand and almost dropped it a few times, which of course earned me a very stern look from my handsome landlord who just so happened to be knowledgeable about littles and daddies.

Was he in the lifestyle?

Well, he must be. After spending just a short time around me, he'd recognized me as a little.

I assumed (seriously hoped) that he didn't already

have a wife or a girlfriend or a little. Surely if he did, he wouldn't be flirting with me so openly right now.

I didn't obey. I kept playing with the spoon and squirming in my seat. Twice, the spoon clattered to the table, and I picked it up before he could snatch it away. I giggled each time he missed.

"That's it, baby girl," he said, raising his voice. But it didn't quite matter since no one was close enough to hear him scolding me. "I've had enough of your deliberate naughtiness. Hand me the spoon right now."

The air between us was thick and charged with tension. Holding the spoon in my right hand, I froze and stared at him with my mouth agape.

What would he do if I didn't give him the spoon? Would he march me out to his truck and give me a spanking? And if so, how would he go about it? I assumed the punishment would happen in his back seat, where the windows were heavily tinted, but would he take me over his knee for a spanking or would he order me to bend over something?

My face heated as I imagined him marching me out to his truck, his face set in a stern expression as he murmured into my ear that he planned to make me one very sorry little girl.

"It's my spoon and you can't have it," I blurted. With a cheeky grin, I resumed twirling the utensil from hand to hand. Occasionally, I paused to take a bite of the pancakes or a sip of coffee. I didn't know a whole lot about being a little, but I knew I was bratting right now. Lightly bratting. And in all the books

I'd read, little girls who bratted most definitely got in trouble with their daddies. They got scolded and spanked. Sometimes they got corner time, too, or even more intimate punishments that made them blush bright red.

Derek straightened in his seat and shot me his sternest look yet. Suddenly, I was very aware of the wetness in my panties. I was getting so achy and wet that I was making a mess. I stopped squirming around and spinning the spoon. What if I soaked through my panties to my dress? Shame heated me all over. That would be the most embarrassing thing ever. Maybe I ought to listen to Derek and settle down. Behave.

Or maybe not.

He reached down to readjust himself in his pants, and not for the first time since we'd sat down for breakfast. It would seem we were both excited.

"If you don't hand me the spoon right now, baby girl," he eventually said, "Daddy is going to punish you. I mean it, Gemma. Do you want a spanking on your bare little bottom?"

His words weren't just a threat, they were a question. And a dare. He was threatening to chastise me if I didn't behave, but he was also *asking* if he could spank me.

If I didn't want a punishment, no big deal. I could just hand over the spoon.

But if I wanted to explore more of this exciting dynamic between us, then he was daring me to misbehave. Daring me to be a naughty baby girl so her daddy would have a reason to spank her.

Well, I knew what I wanted. Before I could over-think things, I flicked the spoon and it clattered to the floor. "Oops."

His eyes flashed and he leaned closer. "Pick it up. Pick it up and put it on the table or the spanking you have coming is going to be so much worse than I'm already planning."

My stomach clenched with nerves and heat shot between my thighs. I stared at him for a moment, stunned that this was actually happening. Not only had I met the stern, cowboy daddy of my dreams, but he kept calling me baby girl, scolding me, and he'd even promised to punish me.

Another tingle raced across my bottom cheeks and the quaking in my privates grew stronger. So strong I had to resist the urge to rub myself between my thighs in the middle of the restaurant.

I bit my lower lip. "Sorry, Derek." *Daddy*. Could I call him that yet?

Thankfully, he saved me from having to ask.

"That's Daddy to you, young lady. Now pick up the spoon. Don't make me ask again."

I rushed to retrieve the spoon from the floor. As I did so, I cast another glance around to make sure we had plenty of privacy. Yep, still pretty much alone. Thank goodness. I liked having Daddy to myself while also in a public place. It added some excitement to the trouble I'd gotten in.

The idea of someone witnessing *Daddy* threaten to punish me was thrilling, even though I didn't actually want anyone to overhear.

"Thank you. Now, finish your breakfast. We're leaving in two minutes." He pulled out his wallet and put a fifty-dollar bill on the table. "You're going to regret your mischief once I get you out to the truck, baby girl. I'm glad you wore a dress. It'll be easy for Daddy to access that naughty bottom of yours."

CHAPTER 8

DEREK

I WISHED I HAD MY TOOL BAG AS I WALKED OUT OF the diner, but fortunately we didn't run into anyone. Good thing, too, because I was packing some serious wood.

I kept a hand to Gemma's lower back as I marched her toward my truck, which was parked in the rear of the otherwise empty lot next to the diner. We would have plenty of privacy for what I had planned.

Once we reached the truck, I turned Gemma in my arms and peered down at her. She was trembling slightly, but her face was flushed, and she was breathing rapidly. She was nervous, but she was also excited about the prospect of receiving her first spanking. A spanking she had practically begged me for as she'd playfully goaded me in the restaurant.

My cock swelled harder as I recalled the way she'd swiped her perfect pink tongue over the spoon. I had several ideas for that tongue of hers, but they would have to wait. I'd promised her a spanking and I was a man of my word.

"You were a very naughty baby girl in the restaurant, Gemma," I said in a strict, scolding tone. "You ought to know better than to misbehave like that, especially in public."

She lowered her head and looked adorably repentant. "Sorry, Daddy," she murmured.

Hearing her call me Daddy for the first time caused my loins to tighten. What was occurring between us was very fast, I knew that, but I also knew it felt natural and right. Easy. As though we were meant to be together.

Love at first sight?

I pushed back a wave of guilt. Logically, I knew there wasn't anything wrong with finding love again. I also knew Trisha wouldn't want me to be alone forever.

I took a deep breath and pushed away thoughts of the past and focused on the mischievous baby girl who was standing in front of me like a gift from the heavens.

"Into the car with you, young lady. You're going to get it." I released her and opened the door, thankful that the windows were darkly tinted. We could see out just fine, but no one would be able to see us unless they pressed their face to the glass. I was also thankful I'd sprung for the extended cab version of this truck. Plenty of room back here to take a naughty girl in hand.

"Yes, Daddy." She crawled into the truck with my assistance.

I slid in next to her, shut the door and locked it. I turned to face her and noticed she was fisting her hands in the skirt of her dress. Fidgeting nervously as she gnawed on her bottom lip and stared at me with wide anxious eyes. She also squirmed a few times, reminding me that her panties were likely soaked with her arousal.

I patted my thigh. "Place yourself over Daddy's lap, little Gemma. You know you have a spanking coming. A quick one in the truck and then once I get you home, you'll be getting a second, much harder one."

She crossed her arms over her chest and stuck her lip out in a cute pout. "Two spankings? Daddy, that's not fair!" She huffed and stomped her foot. "I'm not that naughty. I'm a good girl."

I struggled not to smile at her antics. She was misbehaving, but she was being adorable while she did it. I didn't know whether to tan her hide or kiss her senseless.

I reached for her hair and stroked a hand through her silken locks, and something inside me softened when she leaned into my touch with a soft sigh. "Of course you're a good girl," I said, "but sometimes good girls make mistakes, and when that happens, they need guidance. Correction. In your case, Gemma, I think you will benefit from a spanking."

She looked suddenly hopeful. "Just one spanking?"

I shook my head back and forth slowly. "You're getting a few smacks here in the back of the truck, then once we get home, I'm going to take you over my knee for a longer spanking. Maybe once I'm through reddening your bottom, you'll think twice about misbehaving in public, won't you, young lady?"

She stared at me for a long moment before finally uttering, "Okay, Daddy. I-I'm sorry I was naughty in the restaurant. But please don't spank me too hard. Just a light spanking, Daddy, please please please."

"You'll get whatever I decide you need, young lady." I patted my thigh again. "Now come here. Be an obedient baby girl and place yourself over Daddy's lap."

GEMMA

THE QUAKING IN MY PRIVATES INCREASED WITH every breath, and my whole body trembled as I placed myself over Derek's lap. *Daddy's lap.*

My heart skipped a beat.

He'd told me to call him Daddy. And for real this time, not by mistake.

He guided me farther over his lap, positioning me with my bottom lifted high. Instantly, I detected the hardness in his pants. Wow. Daddy felt huge. Tall and broad-shouldered as he was, I wasn't surprised, but my pulse fluttered as I imagined trying to accept Daddy's big girthy cock in my mouth or... elsewhere.

He smoothed a hand over my bottom, which was still covered by my panties and dress. He'd mentioned something earlier about my dress giving him easy access to my bottom. Did that mean he was going to lift the skirt and spank me over my panties? Or would he also pull my panties down and spank me on the bare bottom?

I shot a nervous glance at the nearest window. I'd misbehaved in public and now Daddy was going to punish me in public. Sort of.

He cupped my ass and gave it a firm squeeze, then he slowly drew the skirt upward, revealing my panty-clad bottom to his gaze. I peered over my shoulder, wanting to see his expression.

To my great embarrassment, he spread my legs wide and leaned down to stare at my crotch.

"May I touch you?" he asked.

I found myself nodding in agreement and quivering in anticipation of his touch.

He swiped a finger over the strip of fabric that covered my privates, and I couldn't help but jerk backward against his hand.

"Just as I suspected." He met my eyes. "You're soaking wet, baby girl."

CHAPTER 9

DEREK

THE SCENT OF GEMMA'S AROUSAL MADE ME
ravenous to claim her. If she knew the full details of
all I wanted to do to her, she would probably run
screaming from the truck.

I needed to take things slow.

Well, slow-ish.

I wanted to earn her trust more than anything. I
wanted to take care of her, give her what she needed.
What she craved. I wanted to watch her squirm over
my lap as I stroked her slick folds and reddened her
bottom.

Her eyes darkened with lust as I continued trailing
a finger over her panty-covered pussy. She turned and
reached frantically around as though searching for
something to grasp onto. Finally, she settled on

placing one hand on my lower leg and the other on the middle seatbelt.

"If you'd been a good girl in the restaurant, Daddy could be giving you nothing but pleasure right now," I said, keeping my touch light. "But instead, you're about to get your bottom spanked. In the back of my truck, no less. Anyone who happens to walk by will know there's a naughty young lady in here getting a sound spanking from her daddy."

A whimper drifted from her throat, and she pushed her ass back toward my hand. The movement caused friction against my rock-hard cock, drawing a moan from me.

"No more moving around," I ordered. "You will remain as still as possible while Daddy punishes you. Remember, you're just getting a few smacks in the truck. Once we get home, then you're really going to get it. I won't stand for my baby girl misbehaving, especially in public. You ought to know better." *My baby girl.* We'd barely gotten started and already I was thinking of her as my baby girl. I very much wanted to drive her home to the ranch rather than back to her brick rental on Main Street.

"I'll try to stay still, Daddy," she said, "but it's difficult when you keep touching my privates and making me feel so good." She glanced over her shoulder at me with a hopeful look, then wiggled her bottom slightly, seductively. "Maybe we could forget all about me being naughty in the restaurant and we could have, um, *other* fun instead. Grown-up fun." She sucked in a shaky breath. "I know you're excited, Daddy. I can feel your big thing beneath me, and it only keeps growing larger and harder."

I withdrew my hand from her center and gave her panty-covered bottom two sharp swats, delivering one to each curvy cheek. "No grown-up fun until you've received your punishment in full, baby girl. That means you'll only receive pleasure once this bottom of yours is well-spanked and bright red. Now stop moving. I'll not warn you again."

"But Daddy—owie owie owwww!!" She squirmed and kicked her feet as I gave her a series of rapid, hard smacks, all delivered overtop her panties.

I paused to massage her cheeks for a moment as she fought to catch her breath. She eventually gave a contented sigh, no doubt believing this spanking was over.

"As naughty as you were in the truck just now, young lady, trying to get out of your spanking, I think you've earned some extra swats. On your bare bottom." I took my time pulling her panties down until they rested just above her knees, nearly groaning at the sight of her slick pink folds. The enticing scent of her arousal made me want to bend her over the center console and plunge into her sweetness from behind. But I refrained from ravishing her, reminding myself that I wanted to earn her trust, wanted her desperate and pleading to be claimed.

Her breath hitched as I stroked her bare flesh and admired the splotch of pink in the center of each punished cheek.

"But Daddy!" she blurted after a few seconds of

rubbing. "Not on my bare bottom! That's not fair! I-I wasn't *that* naughty!"

"I decide what's fair, baby girl, and yes, you were *that* naughty." Before she could protest further, I tightened my hold on her and gave her ten fast spanks, most of them delivered to her vulnerable sit-spot, where her upper thighs curved into her buttocks. I wanted her to feel the heat as we drove back to her place where the final portion of her chastisement would be delivered.

"Ouch, Daddy, that hurt!" She reached back and rubbed her butt, but I swatted her hand away.

"No rubbing, Gemma. You are meant to feel the sting. If I catch you rubbing, you'll be sorry." I ran a hand over her heated flesh once more before slowly pulling her panties up.

My cock thickened further, if that were even possible at this point, as I gazed at the very noticeable wet spot on her crotch.

"So wet and so naughty," I said, running my thumb lightly over the moist scrap of fabric. I delighted in her needy gasp and the way her center undulated in midair as she sought more of my touch only to be left bereft when I withdrew my hand. God, how I liked teasing her.

"Daddy, I-I'm all achy," she said in a little voice. "You know, *down there.*" Her eyes widened as she continued peering at me, her expression urgent and pleading, her face beautifully flushed.

If she were to beg me to claim her at this very moment, I didn't think I would be able to resist. But I fucking needed to get control of myself. Not only was I one of the most well-known residents of Rocky Springs, but I held the livelihood of dozens of people in my hands. One wrong move—like getting arrested for public fornication in the parking lot of Kay's Diner—could put my business in jeopardy and negatively impact those who worked for me. The last thing I needed was a scandal.

I took a few calming breaths and finally lifted the little beauty to sit upon my lap. Her dress fell back into place, and she gave me a bashful look as she squirmed around as though trying to find a more comfortable position. But I knew better. She was teasing me. Pressing her punished bottom down on my hardness.

I grabbed hold of her upper arms and forced her to remain still. When she huffed in protest, I gave her a stern look. "I'm going to drive you home now, Gemma, and once we get home, I think you know what will happen."

She emitted a tiny gasp and her eyes widened. "More spanking?" Her look of nervousness made my cock so fucking hard.

"Yes, baby girl, more spanking." I flicked her nose playfully. "A proper spanking. One that'll leave you sore for quite some time."

I quieted her protests by placing a finger to her lips, effectively shushing her. Then I guided her to sit in the back middle seat and buckled her up before opening the door and stepping out.

"Why can't I sit up front, Daddy?" She pulled at

the seatbelt, but I swatted her hands away from the buckle.

I leaned in so close I could feel the warm puffs of her breath. She stared at me unblinkingly as I gave her thigh a quick squeeze. "Because you're a baby girl and baby girls are supposed to sit in the backseat. It's safer there, and I want to keep you safe."

"You do?" The sudden look of longing in her dark, expressive eyes reflected my own deep desires for a partner.

I swallowed past the burning in my throat and nodded. "Yes, little one, I do." Before the interaction could go any further, I closed the back door and got behind the wheel.

CHAPTER 10

GEMMA

I COULDN'T STOP SQUIRMING IN THE SEAT. THE aching in my core was so intense I couldn't stand it. I needed relief. Not another spanking.

Although, if I were being honest, the reason I was becoming increasingly excited and breathless was the knowledge that I had another spanking coming. And not just any spanking, but a *proper spanking*. Derek—*Daddy's*—words from moments ago replayed in my head.

Proper spanking sounded serious, though I wasn't certain of all it would entail. He'd mentioned taking me over his knee for a longer spanking, one that would no doubt be delivered on my bare bottom.

Would he scold me again? Would he order me to stand in the corner and think about my actions?

Would he touch me *down there* after the spanking was over?

A fresh ache pulsed between my thighs, one so intense I couldn't help but try to assuage the incessant throbbing. Keeping one eye on Daddy (I didn't want him to catch me in the act, how embarrassing!), I slowly reached a hand up my dress. My thighs quivered as I pressed a finger directly to my clit, though I touched myself over my panties.

I pressed my lips tightly together to keep from making any noises. A moan built in my throat, but I held back, not wanting to alert Daddy to my naughtiness. Well, I didn't know for sure that I was breaking his rules, but I suspected he would consider me touching myself a big no no.

In all the daddy dom romances I'd read, little girls who touched their privates without permission got into major trouble with their daddies. I was nervous enough about the spanking I had coming, and I didn't want to incur any additional punishments. I recalled a novel I'd read where the daddy had smacked his little girls' pussy lips a dozen times after he'd caught her pleasuring herself without permission. My pulse spiked and my blood heated, and the warm tremors between my thighs deepened.

I rubbed myself harder, faster.

But then I made a big mistake.

I released a half-gasp, half-moan, and when I glanced into the rearview mirror to see if Daddy had noticed my activities, my eyes instantly met with an icy blue glare.

Uh oh. A quiver shot across my bottom cheeks, and I wrenched my hand out from underneath my dress. My face heated with shame over having been caught.

"Absolutely not. No touching yourself, young lady," Daddy said in a scolding tone. "Not without permission. You ought to know better."

"Sorry, Daddy," I murmured. "I couldn't help it. I-I am just so achy and unsettled." My face grew hotter still.

"Place your hands atop your head for the remainder of the car ride," he ordered.

I was quick to comply and laced my fingers together behind my head. Would my mistake earn me extra punishment? As I imagined all the things Daddy might do to me once he got me home, my breasts started to feel heavy, and my nipples tightened. I was starting to ache all over it would seem.

"Good. Now keep your hands just like that. If you move them for even a second, young lady, I will pull the truck over and redden your bottom good, right on the side of the road."

His threat caused warmth to pang in my center. I tried very hard not to squirm around in the seat. The last thing I wanted to do was make Daddy any more cross with me.

Excitement rippled through me as he pulled into the driveway of my new home. He'd been parked on the street in front of the house earlier, but I liked that he was parking in the driveway next to my car. For a brief second, I imagined that we lived together and were just coming home from breakfast and running errands. Normal couple stuff.

He opened the door and reached over me to unfasten my seatbelt, and I took advantage of his sudden nearness and inhaled deeply of his pleasing masculine scent. Satisfaction filled me when I noticed the massive bulge in his pants.

But just as he assisted me in stepping down from the truck, a tractor trailer came to a stop in front of the house. The horn beeped twice and a man in the passenger seat waved at us.

I tried to fight back the frustration that swept through me at the movers' inconvenient timing. I waved back at the moving men and then turned to face Derek. Daddy. Hm. Should I think of him as Derek right now? Well, I knew I couldn't call him Daddy in front of other people. That much was obvious.

I sighed as he gave my hand an affectionate squeeze, and my heart instantly softened toward him. He could no doubt sense my frustration and he was trying to comfort me. Even though I was certain he must be pretty frustrated himself right about now.

"They weren't supposed to be here until around noon," I said with another sigh. "I'm sorry." What would happen now? Would Derek leave and forget all about the proper spanking he'd promised me? My spirits sank at the thought of him leaving.

"Hey, baby girl," he whispered, "you don't need to apologize. You also don't need to look so sad. I'm not going anywhere, and as soon as I get you alone, you're going to get that proper spanking I promised you."

"Oh? *Really?*" I swallowed hard and glanced over my shoulder briefly as the movers crawled out of the truck. I returned my gaze to Derek and took comfort in the heated look in his eyes.

He turned me around and gave my bottom a playful swat, then he leaned down and placed his lips at my ear. A delightful shiver rushed through me as his warm breath tickled my face and neck.

"Yes, *really*, baby girl. Now try to behave yourself while the movers are here. Company or not, if I catch you rubbing your privates again without permission, I will march you upstairs and give you a sound spanking."

I gasped and turned to meet Daddy's stern gaze. The idea of the movers hearing me get a spanking from my daddy left me aching and trembling with desire.

"Be good, baby girl," he said in a warning tone, "or else."

CHAPTER 11

DEREK

Gemma shot me a mischievous glance as I retrieved the tool bag from the back of my truck. "I thought you'd already finished installing the trim," she said with a giggle just as the movers approached.

I suppressed the urge to growl at her.

Think PG thoughts, Bolt.

If I could get my dick under control, I could help the movers unload the truck and get them on their way sooner. The need to be alone with Gemma consumed me. I couldn't stop thinking about scolding her, taking her over my knee, and pulling her panties down to reveal her cute little bottom.

So much for PG thoughts. Good thing my tool bag was large, though I probably looked like an idiot holding it in front of my crotch.

Pleasantries were exchanged with the movers, and

Gemma soon opened the front door and showed them where to place the boxes. From what I understood, today's delivery contained her supplies for the art studio she planned to open.

After fidgeting around for a few minutes as I pretended I was looking for something in the back of my truck, my cock finally softened enough that I was able to assist the movers. In just over an hour, we had the back of the truck unloaded.

I couldn't help but marvel at how confident Gemma appeared as she flitted about the meeting hall area of the house, asking the movers to place this box here and that box there, and starting to arrange the room just the way she liked it. There were a few pieces of furniture as well that needed placing, and she didn't seem reluctant to ask the movers to put the items just where she wanted them.

Her enthusiasm was contagious, and when I saw her pull the first painting from a large box, my mouth dropped open and I stared in admiration at the beautiful abstract painting of snow-capped mountains.

"You did this?" I asked.

She beamed up at me. "Yep." She passed me the painting. "Would you mind putting this on the large easel near the window facing the street, please?

I flashed her a smile and went off to do her bidding, while she rushed outside to thank the movers. I noticed her passing them each a wad of cash and then waving as they pulled away.

I met her at the doorway and drew her into my arms, not caring if anyone walking down the street witnessed the affection I was showing her. I couldn't resist the urge to hold her, the need to feel her leaning against me. She froze for a moment and gave me a strange look but eventually sank deeper into my arms with a soft sigh. I stroked a hand through her silken hair and inhaled the floral scent of her shampoo.

"Thanks for helping," she said. "I can't wait to get my studio up and running. If everything goes to plan, I ought to be ready to open in about two weeks."

"Are you waiting on another shipment?" I pulled back and stared into her soulful dark eyes. I liked seeing her excited and animated. But I also couldn't help but wonder about her exact reasons for moving all the way to Rocky Springs from Connecticut.

She nodded. "I arranged to have a sign installed out front, and I ordered some touristy doodads to sell in addition to my paintings. You know, magnets, mugs, and t-shirts that have my designs on them. I could do a soft opening now, sure, but I think I want to wait until the store is totally perfect. Also, I want to host paint nights here once or twice a month, so I need to get that organized and make some flyers. Gotta finish updating my website too." She laughed. "I might need more than two cups of coffee every day if I'm going to get all this done in two weeks."

"Well, I don't know much about designing websites," I said, "but I'd be happy to help you finish unpacking and setting up your studio. Also happy to help you spread flyers all over town."

She gave me a skeptical look. "We, um, just met, and don't you have a lot of work yourself? I know you own Rocky Springs Ranch and Resort." She glanced through the window at my truck where the ranch's logo was plastered on the side.

"I don't run the ranch all on my own," I said in a reassuring tone. "I have plenty of people that work for me and if I take a day off here and there it's not a big deal. Besides, you're my newest tenant. One could argue it's my job to help you get settled in your new place. Now, as for us just having met…" My voice trailed off and I fumbled for words.

"Yes? About that part?" She lifted her eyebrows slightly, giving me a questioning look. A hopeful look.

I cupped her face in my hands and brushed my thumbs over her flushed cheeks. "There's something about you, baby girl. I have never, ever, spanked a woman in the back of my truck only two hours after meeting her. I also haven't gone on a date—yes, breakfast out counts as a date—in several years. I've been alone for a long time, too long, but with you… well, there's an instant attraction. I want to get to know you better, little one, and I hope you'll agree to spend more time with me."

Her lips parted on a tiny gasp, and a look of immense longing brimmed in her eyes. I didn't know much about her yet, but I sensed she was as lonely as I was. But when I was in her presence, she filled up the empty places in my soul.

It was as though I *recognized her*.

As though I'd known her in a past life or something.

God, how could I explain it without sounding unhinged?

Her lips curved in a slight smile, and she stood on her tiptoes as she wrapped her arms around my neck, which forced me to bend down. My gaze instantly went to her mouth.

GEMMA

DEREK'S WORDS RESONATED DEEP INSIDE ME. HE was saying all the right things. Hadn't I longed for a man who would understand me and accept my little side? Knowing he wanted to spend more time with me made me want to cry tears of joy.

He pulled me a few steps away from the door and pushed it shut, affording us complete privacy. Alone. We were alone together at last.

Daddy. He was a daddy. A sexy, dominant cowboy who'd already spanked me and saw me half-naked in the process. Funny how we'd skipped to second (or was it third?) base without even kissing yet. But I planned to rectify that soon. I kept my arms around his neck and parted my lips as his mouth hovered but two inches from mine.

I drew in a deep breath, my eyes not leaving his. "I would love to spend more time with you. Daddy. I, um, can't stop thinking about your earlier comment. That maybe this is fate. Is that weird? Are we moving too fast? I don't even know what your favorite color is or what kind of condiments you like on a hot dog or if you—"

He leaned forward and silenced me with a kiss, and I forgot what I'd been about to say. Something about how little we actually knew about each other. But it didn't matter. Not now. All that mattered was that he kept holding me and kissing me. Oh yes. Just like that. I moaned into his mouth as he swept his tongue softly against mine.

He shifted his hands behind my head and tangled his fingers in my hair as he deepened the kiss. My mind spun and there was a moment where I was certain I must be floating. As Daddy kissed me, he pressed his groin against my lower stomach, allowing me to feel his hardness. A heated quiver rushed through me, and I found myself undulating my hips toward him.

I couldn't say how long the kiss lasted. A few seconds, or maybe an hour. I wasn't sure. All I knew was that it felt as though the world had stopped spinning. When he finally pulled his lips from mine, I was panting breathlessly and there was a fervent ache building between my thighs.

His eyes were glazed over with passion, but his visage all at once became stern, causing flutters to rise in my tummy. The spanking. He hadn't yet given me that proper spanking he'd promised. My butt was still stinging from the couple of smacks he'd given me in the back of his truck, but a real spanking... could I take it?

"I know we don't know one another well yet, baby girl," he said in a voice that reminded me of melted caramel, "but I am asking you to trust me to give you what you need. I realize you're new to being a little girl and you've never had a daddy before, but I promise I'll go slow and help to guide you."

Trust. I wanted to trust him. Desperately so. The loneliness of the past year had nearly broken me. The scandal in my hometown had also caused me to lose most of my friends, people I'd thought I could trust. People I'd thought would have my back no matter what. But I reminded myself that I still had a few friends. Not everyone was judgmental or untrustworthy.

I placed a hand on Derek's chest. "I trust you so far," I said. He hadn't yet done anything to make me believe he couldn't be trusted. I felt safe with him, and I wanted so badly to believe meeting him was indeed fate that I was willing to give him the benefit of the doubt. Until he proved otherwise, I would trust that he was a good person. Someone I could safely explore my little side with.

He smoothed a hand through my hair and glanced at the stairs before returning his gaze to mine. "I'm glad you trust me so far, little one. I promise I'll try my best not to do anything to break your trust. Trust is the foundation of a little's relationship with her daddy."

My throat closed up and I couldn't reply right away. So I nodded and tried to regain control of my emotions. I didn't want to break down in tears, even if they weren't tears of sadness, right now. I wanted to go upstairs with Daddy and explore more of our… relationship.

Well, he'd used that word first, so I might as well use it too.

Fast. So fast. Panic crept in as I thought about how fast things were moving between us. What if I fell head over heels for Derek and then he broke my heart? This town was supposed to be my fresh start. The last thing I needed was to fuck that up. I wanted to belong here. But how could I belong if I had a falling out with Derek Bolt, rancher and landlord extraordinaire?

"What are you thinking about right now?" he asked, shifting me in his arms. He rubbed his hands up and down my back as he held me close, but not close enough that he couldn't peer down into my eyes.

I shrugged one shoulder. "I'm thinking about all the things that might go wrong. What if… what if this ends up being a mistake?"

A look of understanding came over him, and he eventually graced me with a smile that revealed those sexy dimples of his. "What about all the things that might go right?"

CHAPTER 12

DEREK

AFTER MAKING SURE GEMMA WAS WILLING AND ready, I guided her upstairs to her apartment, holding her trembling hand tightly in mine.

I led her into the kitchen and drew a straight-backed chair into the middle of the room. She swallowed hard and her cheeks grew pinker. Her eyes widened as she watched me methodically roll up the sleeves of my flannel shirt.

"You're adorable when you blush, baby girl." I sank down on the chair and pulled her to stand between my spread legs, finally dropping her hand. "And I have a feeling you'll be blushing a lot more by the time I'm through with you. I intend to be thorough as I punish you."

She lowered her head and peeked at me from beneath thick dark lashes. She twisted her fingers together and stepped from foot to foot in a nervous manner that caused all the blood in my body to rush straight to my dick. I hardened painfully in my pants, and not for the first time in Gemma's presence I resisted the urge to readjust myself.

"You were naughty in the restaurant, weren't you, baby girl?" I asked in a scolding but imploring tone.

"Yes, Daddy, I-I was naughty in the restaurant." She gnawed on her bottom lip and gave me a worried look. "Sorry about that, Daddy."

"You were also naughty in the truck, young lady," I continued in a sharp tone. "You tried to bribe your way out of a spanking. You tried to tempt Daddy into grown-up fun so you could get out of your punishment, didn't you?"

"I, um, yes," she said after a long pause. "But Daddy, I couldn't help it. I was so achy *down there*. In my privates. I wanted you to touch me. I wanted you to help make me feel good." She kept stepping from foot to foot and pressing her thighs together, no doubt in an effort to relieve the worst of her aching.

"If you're obedient during your spanking, baby girl, and accept your punishment without too much fuss, Daddy will touch your privates and make you feel good afterward." I reached under her dress, forced her legs apart, and trailed my fingers along the crotch of her panties.

She jerked forward with a whimper and placed her hands on my shoulders to keep from falling over. "Okay, Daddy," she said, "I promise I'll be good during my spanking." Once I helped steady her, she let go of my shoulders and stood on her own again, though she continued fidgeting.

She was shaking with a combination of desire and nerves, and her nonstop blushes made her appear almost feverish. My cock stiffened when I recalled the scent of her arousal in the truck. I couldn't wait to strip off her panties and smell her excitement again. Couldn't wait to redden that cute bottom of hers and then stroke her to bliss.

What sorts of noises would she make as she came? God, I couldn't wait to find out. I imagined she would whimper and moan as I rubbed her clit, and maybe cry out louder during an actual climax.

I patted my thigh. "It's time for your spanking, baby girl. Please place yourself over Daddy's lap."

She gave me a dubious look but soon complied, stepping to my side and then lowering herself across my thighs. The extra pressure this placed on my engorged shaft tore a groan from my throat before I could stop it. I cupped her bottom overtop her dress and spent a few seconds massaging her cheeks. She sighed and grabbed hold of my leg to steady herself, and I took the opportunity to position her ass higher upon my lap. Next, I lifted her dress and slowly pulled her panties down, leaving them to rest at her knees just as I had in the truck.

I touched the center of each of her cheeks, pressing just hard enough to reinvigorate the sting of her earlier spanking. She gasped and shifted over my lap, but she didn't attempt to escape. Such a good, obedient baby girl she was, keeping in position as she awaited her punishment.

"Just a bit red," I said, stroking her ass. "But not red enough. By the time I'm through with you, young lady, your bottom will be glowing."

She sucked in a shaky breath and peered over her shoulder at me, her wide dark eyes glinting with fear. "Daddy? Um, how bad is it going to hurt?"

Holding her gaze, I cupped her bottom gently. "I know this is your first spanking, sweet one, and I promise I won't take it too far. It will hurt, but not too badly. Trust me to give you what you need, Gemma." The responsibility to guide her fell upon my shoulders, but it wasn't an unwelcome weight. Her care and her comfort, even during a well-earned punishment, remained at the forefront of my mind.

She worried her lower lip for a few seconds and finally nodded, then turned and settled back into place. Her lower stomach pressed upon my hardening cock, causing a jolt of sensation to rush up my thighs. My balls tightened with desire, and I felt hot all over despite the cool breeze entering through an open kitchen window.

I placed a firm hand to her lower back and lifted my other hand, preparing my aim. *Crack!* My palm impacted upon her left cheek. A weak smack, all things considered. It didn't even draw a gasp of surprise from her. But I'd meant for the slap to be faint. A few tiny smacks, then a few slightly harder ones, until I worked her up to the point where I could administer the hardest blows yet.

I continued spanking her, alternating from cheek to cheek, landing light slaps on her bare bottom. Though I was being gentle, the color of her flesh gradually turned pinker. Eventually, I worked her up to the medium impact smacks, and these finally caused her to gasp and squirm over my lap. But she wasn't trying to escape, and I sensed that she was doing her best to remain as still as possible. Her obedience pleased me.

"Look at this naughty baby girl," I said, continuing with her punishment as I dispensed a few smacks to her sit-spot. "Over her daddy's lap getting her bare bottom spanked. I bet you'll think twice about misbehaving the next time we go out in public, won't you, young lady?"

"Oh! Owie! Um, yes, Daddy! I'll be good next time." As she shifted over my lap, her thighs opened enough that I could glimpse the gleaming pink lips of her pussy. There was no hiding it. My baby girl was becoming aroused during her punishment. Perhaps some of her squirming around was due to the achiness between her thighs rather than the pain of her spanking.

I paused in smacking her reddened bottom and forced her thighs wider apart. I wanted to grab hold of her cheeks and spread them wide enough to reveal her puckering hole, but I fought the urge to do so. We were already moving fast, and I didn't want to scare her away. I wanted to see her again and again. I wanted to pack up her boxes and move her out to my ranch.

Possessive. I already felt so possessive of her, I didn't know how I would part with her when evening came and I needed to return home to my ranch. I shoved aside this worry and refocused my attention on the matter at hand—the errant baby girl who was over my lap, her bottom glowing, her thighs parted to reveal her slick, swollen nether lips.

"You have five smacks left, Gemma, and they will be the hardest yet. You'll receive them just like this—with your legs spread wide. Daddy wants to keep looking at your privates as he spanks you."

She nodded and murmured something I didn't quite catch, and my cock thickened further as I took in the sight of her punished cheeks and her gleaming pussy. She was completely bare between her legs.

I gave her the final five spanks in rapid succession, and true to my word, they were the hardest yet. Each one drew a shocked gasp from her and caused her to squirm more fervently upon my lap. But once I'd delivered the last one, I cupped her bottom and massaged her stinging cheeks. The glimmer of moisture between her thighs increased as I rubbed her punished flesh, and a few whimpers and moans drifted from her throat.

She drew in a deep breath and turned to peer over her shoulder at me. An urgent, needy look entered her eyes. "Please, Daddy," she said with a whimper. "Please, will you touch me? Down there? Will you help the aching in my privates go away? *Please?*"

CHAPTER 13

GEMMA

I was consumed with desire. Urgent, achy, ceaseless desire. My bottom cheeks hurt, though not too badly. The sting coalesced with the aching in my center, causing my clit to throb harder. If Daddy didn't do something about it soon, I wouldn't be able to stop myself from reaching between my thighs.

When I felt his hand nudging my legs apart, then the tips of his fingers drifting over my pussy, I almost sobbed with relief. *Oh yes. Touch me, Daddy. Rub my privates. Please.*

I lifted my center against his probing hand. Whimpers left me when he dipped inside my core and drew my moisture outward, spreading it over my swollen clit.

"Is this what my baby girl wants?" His deep voice

vibrated through me, and I lifted my bottom higher, inviting more of his touch.

"Yes, Daddy. Please don't stop."

His fingers danced along the seam of my nether lips and over my clit, which I realized must be so swollen it was protruding from my folds. I flushed and wondered what he must think of my heightened state of arousal. I'd never been so achy and wet and turned on in my life. I felt like one of the heroines in the daddy dom romances I liked to read before bed each night. I'd felt that way ever since Derek had said, 'You can call me Daddy.'

Well, a few hours later and not only was I calling him Daddy, but I'd allowed him to spank me and touch my privates.

The pleasure built as he continued rubbing my moisture overtop my pulsing nubbin. I gasped and tried to catch my breath. Blissful sensations coursed through me, and I felt momentarily dizzy, never mind that I wasn't even standing up.

He dipped two fingers—or maybe it was three, I couldn't be sure—into my core again and proceeded to spread my moisture outward, covering my clit with another layer of my arousal. I jerked against his touch and cried out. He swirled a digit over my nubbin and pressed harder, and kept going and going until...

Dark spots dotted my vision and a wave of ecstasy crashed over me. I groaned, undulating my hips as I shamelessly ground my center back into his hand. As the last vestiges of my release faded, I struggled to hold my head up, I was so drained of energy.

I was vaguely aware of Daddy lifting me and turning me over to sit on his lap. He wrapped his arms around me, holding and steadying me at the same time. He pressed his warm lips to my forehead, and I absolutely melted. The comfort he was showing me, as well as the affection, brought tears to my eyes.

For the first time in my life, I felt like a baby girl who was truly cherished by her daddy. I wished I could stay here like this forever, sitting on his lap while he rubbed my back and kissed my forehead. I felt safe and treasured in his arms.

I realized the spanking he'd just given me wasn't a true punishment spanking—I supposed what had occurred between us thus far could be classified as over-the-top flirting and sexy role playing—but it still felt like one of the most momentous occasions of my life. Because until now, I'd only read about daddy doms and littles and age play relationships. I'd never experienced it personally.

He'd given me a sample of the world I'd been eager to taste.

I was ravenous for more.

What would it be like to receive a true punishment spanking from Daddy? What would it be like to have him as my permanent Daddy?

He pulled back slightly and gazed into my eyes, and I flushed with embarrassment when my bottom lip quivered and a few tears spilled down my cheeks. I wanted to get control of myself. I didn't want him thinking me weak, nor did I want him worrying that he'd hurt me. Both spankings he'd given me had stung, and sitting was a bit uncomfortable at the moment, but neither had hurt enough to make me cry.

"Hey, baby girl," he said in a deep, gentle voice. "Are you okay?"

I sniffled and tried to force a smile, but it wouldn't come. I felt my face crumple as more tears cascaded down my cheeks. Oh no. No no no. The last thing I wanted was to break down sobbing in front of him.

"I'm fine," I said. "Really. I-I am not entirely sure why I'm crying. I suppose I'm just a bit happy and overwhelmed and... well, I'm experiencing a lot of emotions right now." I finally managed a smile even though tears were still escaping my eyes.

He gave me a look of profound understanding that made me melt just as much as that gentle kiss to my forehead had. He could be a strict daddy, but he was also a sweet and caring daddy. He was so freaking perfect that I didn't think any man I encountered from here on out would compare.

Did the handsome cowboy have any idea that in one short day he'd managed to ruin me for all other men?

He gathered me close, pressing my face to his chest, and stroked a hand through my hair as he hugged me. I breathed deep of his masculine scent and reveled in the warmth of his protective embrace. A few more tears rolled down my cheeks in secret.

"It's perfectly normal to be feeling a vast range of emotions right now, baby girl. You just got your first spanking. From a daddy. Tell me, are you having second thoughts about being a little? It's okay if you are, and it would be normal if you were suddenly doubting yourself. Especially when you have a stinging bottom."

I snuggled deeper in his arms. My eyes no longer burned, and my throat didn't feel very tight anymore. I'd finally stopped crying. I sighed and shifted in his embrace to wrap my arms around his waist. I hugged him back and was conscious of the hardness beneath my sore butt. Daddy was still big and firm and excited.

Once I finished processing his words, I said, "I'm not having second thoughts about being a little. But I wasn't expecting to meet someone like you anytime soon. This is all happening so fast." I grinned against his chest. "My plan was to move to Rocky Springs, set up my art studio, and then maybe after a couple of months of settling in and getting my bearings, I would place a very specific personal ad on a dating app looking for a daddy."

He pulled back and shot me a concerned look. "A dating app? Like the kind where people swipe right when they want to bone you?" He gave his head a slow shake. "I've seen news stories about those sorts of apps and I don't think they are very safe. Someone might take advantage of you. Someone might even hurt you." A glint of fury sparked in his eyes, taking me aback. But I wasn't frightened, because I understood he wasn't upset with me but rather the idea of someone hurting me. The realization had me reeling with shocked happiness.

"Well," I said, holding his gaze as a bout of

mischief took hold of me, "if it makes you feel any better, Daddy, if I saw your pic on a dating app, I'd totally swipe right."

He smiled and leaned in to kiss me.

78

CHAPTER 14

DEREK

I HANDED GEMMA ITEMS FROM THE BAGS AND watched as she bustled around the kitchen putting the groceries away. Just as I'd gotten curious looks in Kay's Diner this morning, I'd gotten plenty of stares while in the grocery store with Gemma. Though to the credit of all the busybodies who'd been staring, they'd all watched my interactions with Gemma with hopeful expressions. Everyone in Rocky Springs knew what had happened to Trisha, knew that I'd been alone since her untimely passing.

More than once over the years, a well-meaning friend or acquaintance would comment that I ought to consider dating again. The foreman of my ranch, Burt, had not so inconspicuously introduced me to his sister a couple of weeks ago, and the postal carrier had made numerous comments about how pretty and educated her daughters were.

While I'd been lonely since Trisha's passing, I hadn't actively considered dating again until I'd glimpsed sweet little Gemma standing in her bedroom doorway this morning. One look at her and suddenly I felt open to the possibility that maybe, just maybe, I could start to move on. Maybe I wasn't meant to be alone forever.

I helped Gemma fold the now empty reusable grocery bags and place them in a drawer. She leaned against the counter and crossed her arms over her chest as she gazed around the kitchen with an air of satisfaction.

"Thanks for helping me shop," she said. "It was nice having a big, tall strapping cowboy to reach the top shelves in the grocery store." She shot me a playful look as I walked closer. "I, um, I've enjoyed spending the day with you, Derek-er-Daddy." A blush suffused her cheeks and her lips parted slightly, drawing my eyes to her mouth. My cock stiffened at the thought of kissing her again.

I placed my hands on the counter on either side of her and leaned in close to take a deep inhale of her sweet, feminine scent. I didn't know what kind of shampoo she used, but it was officially my new favorite scent. Lavender and vanilla and something else I couldn't quite place.

"I was happy to help, darlin'," I said, my lips hovering just before hers.

She took in a shaky breath. "So, uh, what happens

now? Are we going to see one another again? Or should I go ahead and join one of those dating apps?" she asked in a teasing tone. A small giggle bubbled up from her chest—no doubt she found my sudden frown amusing.

Raw, savagely possessive urges assailed me. I wanted to grasp her shoulders hard, shake her, and matter-of-factly inform her that she now belonged to me. I wanted to threaten to tan her hide if she even thought about downloading one of those apps to her phone. And yes, I still wanted to take her home with me to the ranch.

"Of course we're going to see one another again, baby girl." I pressed a soft, brief kiss to her lips. "I plan on seeing you tomorrow and the next day, and the day after that too, and so on. I daresay you're going to have a difficult time getting rid of me."

Her eyes filled with hope. "This is going to sound incredibly awkward, but does this mean we're like boyfriend and girlfriend? Or, um, Daddy and little girl? Or do you have other women or littles you play with sometimes? Or do you—"

"There's no one else but you, Gemma," I said, cutting her off. "I already told you I haven't been on a date in years. Remember?"

"Well, a date is one thing and playing with some-one, you know, role play or whatever you want to call it, is different. Just because you've never gone out in public with a woman in years doesn't mean you haven't been having any fun." She flushed an even deeper shade of pink.

I grasped her chin between two fingers and lifted her face upward. "You and I are officially exclusive. Starting now. Do you understand me?"

The hopefulness in her eyes increased. "Yes, Daddy."

"Good. And to answer your question, you're the first woman I've spent any romantic time with in years."

"What about kinky time?"

I almost coughed. "That includes kinky time. First woman, period, in a long, long time." I hoped she wouldn't ask why I'd spent so long celibate and alone. "I guess you could say I've been waiting on the right girl to come along," I added, and it wasn't a lie.

She gave me a curious look that put a knot in my stomach. "You're a lot older than me. Have you ever been... married?"

Coldness washed over me and I released her chin. I took two steps back and leaned against the kitchen island. What should I tell her? Before I could decide what to do, the phone in my pocket buzzed for the tenth time in the last couple of minutes. I hadn't answered it the first nine times, but maybe I ought to answer it now. Someone clearly needed to reach me, and I happened to need a distraction.

I made a show of looking concerned as I pulled the phone from my pocket and stared at the screen. "It's my foreman and he's been calling me repeatedly. I should probably take this."

"Oh, of course! No worries. I'll just finish tidying the kitchen. If you need some privacy, feel free to go downstairs or step outside." She offered me a polite smile that looked a little forced. There was an undeniable awkwardness between us now, but I wasn't yet ready to tell her about Trisha.

"Thanks for understanding," I said. "I'll just step outside quickly."

I rushed downstairs, feeling somewhat like a coward. I'd had no problem flirting with Gemma, kissing her, spanking her, and telling her that we were now exclusively seeing one another.

Why had I hesitated to tell her about Trisha?

Once I reached the front porch, I swiped the answer button and put the phone to my ear. "Hello, Burt. What can I do for you?"

"Derek. We might have a problem. Two of the guests staying on the ranch apparently went out hiking early this morning and they haven't returned yet. They didn't tell our staff where they were going, but two other guests saw them headed for the northern trail just after breakfast."

I growled. "The northern trail? That's supposed to be closed. Did someone remove the warning signs?" Only four days ago, several bears had been spotted feasting on the carcass of a moose just a quarter of a mile from a section of this trail.

"Nope, the signs are still there, as are the logs I dragged across the beginning of the trail. They stepped over the logs and walked right by the "trail closed/bears in the area" signs. Fucking idiot tourists. No doubt they deliberately went that way hoping for a glimpse of a bear and some photos for social media.

I've had the boys out with me looking for them all afternoon. We've ridden the trail five times and haven't spotted them. So, wherever they are, they walked off the main path."

Shit. I rubbed a hand over my face in frustration and turned to face the door. Gemma. I'd hoped to spend the rest of the day with her. But Burt had an emergency on his hands, and I couldn't in good conscience not help him look for the missing guests. As annoyed as I was at the guests for ignoring the 'trail closed' signs, I didn't wish any harm to come upon them. Guests getting mauled by bears would also be incredibly bad for business.

"All right, Burt," I said with a groan, "I'll be there in twenty minutes."

CHAPTER 15

GEMMA

A second after I'd asked Derek if he'd been married before, I'd known his answer, even though he hadn't given one. His phone had buzzed, and he'd had an emergency at the ranch, which had saved him from having to answer me.

Lots of people got divorced, no big deal, and I was just trying to get to know him better. So why would he freeze up and look so sad and hesitant to answer my question? I'd told him a little about my past. Okay, not my big dark secret, but I'd told him about my ex-boyfriend and how we'd broken up because the douche canoe had thought I was disgusting after I confessed my daddy dom fantasies to him.

I glanced at my phone and frowned. Derek and I hadn't exchanged numbers yet. I couldn't even call him. But before he'd rushed off to deal with an emergency on his ranch, he'd claimed he wanted to see me tomorrow. Oh how that pronouncement had lifted my spirits and filled me with hope.

It's not as though he doesn't know where you live, I told myself. *Maybe he'll just show up out of the blue tomorrow and whisk you off for pancakes and coffee.*

My face heated as I recalled the intimacies we'd shared. Not only had he spanked me—*twice!*—but he'd touched my pussy and stroked me to ecstasy. He'd made me come. Hard. I was still feeling a bit breathless and weak in the knees from the pleasure he'd given me.

I'd felt the huge erection in his pants as I'd sat on his lap. I'd expected he might unzip his pants, free his manhood, and instruct me to pleasure him in return. Not only had I expected it, but I'd wanted it. Craved it. As I'd been sitting on his lap, all I could think about was what it would be like to take him in my mouth.

But instead, he'd suggested we go grocery shopping, saying he wanted to make sure my kitchen was fully stocked. While I appreciated his help and I was glad I didn't have to carry all those bags upstairs by myself, now that he was gone, I couldn't help but wish we'd spent that time doing other things. Grown-up things.

A steady, aching pulse affected my center as I imagined Daddy without his clothes on.

If I touched myself right now, would I be breaking his rules? If I confessed having touched myself when he came over tomorrow, would he scold me and give me another spanking?

I sighed and ran a hand through my hair, then padded to my bedroom and opened up my laptop. There was a bit of a mystery surrounding Derek Bolt and I intended to get to the bottom of things. A man as prominent as him would probably be very easy to Google. Maybe I could find out why he'd hesitated to answer me when I'd asked about any previous marriages.

What I discovered both shocked and saddened me.

Poor Derek. Poor Daddy.

I poured over a series of articles from the Rocky Springs Daily. Articles about his late wife, Trisha Bolt, who'd perished in a tragic car accident over five years ago. According to the articles, she'd taken a turn too fast in the rain and spun across the road as a tractor trailer was coming down the mountain in the opposite direction. She'd died instantly. Oh how terribly sad.

Had Daddy really been alone since then?

Was I the first woman he'd spent time with in a romantic and/or kinky way? And if so, why now and why me?

I also looked up his business and read a little bit about Rocky Springs Ranch and Resort. It was a highly rated resort that offered a ranch experience. Guests could ride horses on mountain trails, help with cattle drives, or simply go hiking or kayaking. The resort also had a massive in-ground heated pool, and each guest cabin contained a hot tub. It looked both rustic and luxurious. Wow. I was impressed.

One article I found described Derek Bolt as a rags-to-riches story. Apparently, he'd grown up in poverty and later worked as a ranch hand on a nearby ranch. In time, he'd become the foreman of this ranch, and he'd saved every dime he earned for ten years until he was able to afford the down payment on the land he would eventually turn into Rocky Springs Ranch and Resort.

According to the most recent article, his ranch had just celebrated its ten-year anniversary. There were a few quotes from locals about Derek and his ranch in some of the articles, and all of them were overwhelmingly positive. He'd bought up and repaired numerous buildings on Main Street to help draw new businesses in. Everyone in Rocky Springs seemed to adore him and credited him with single-handedly turning around the economy of the once dilapidated town.

My crush on him increased tenfold. Not because he was wealthy, but because he was a very giving person. He knew what it was like to struggle, and he seemed to like to help others.

And he also happened to be a sexy as fuck daddy dom.

I shut my laptop and went to the large bedroom window that had a view of the mountains. The sun was starting to set, and the horizon was painted with oranges and pinks.

Five years. I couldn't stop thinking about it. Five

years was such a long time. And Daddy had been alone that whole time.

I glanced at his business card. Well, I supposed I had his phone number after all. But I doubted it was his personal cell phone number on that business card. Probably just the main line to the ranch.

I wished I could call him and hear his voice. I wished I could tell him how sorry I was about his wife. Would it upset him to know I'd done some internet sleuthing?

Suddenly, my stomach dropped to my feet and cold terror washed through me.

What if he decided to Google *my name?* Gemma Wilder wasn't a totally uncommon name, but if he searched "artist" along with my name and "Connecticut," where he knew I was from, he would most certainly find a few newspaper articles about me. I cringed as I remembered some of the headlines: *Local Woman Takes Ex to Court over Revenge Porn, Artist Gemma Wilder Closes Studio, Man Sentenced to One Year Probation in Revenge Porn Case,* and *Former Teacher Ordered to Pay Victim $50,000 in Revenge Porn Case.*

And just like that, he would easily know why I'd fled my hometown. Why I'd moved over two thousand miles from where I'd grown up. Why I'd lost most of my friends and why I was estranged from my family. Why my life was one big fucking mess, and why I was desperate to start over.

The intimate pictures of me that Kenny had blasted all over the internet were no longer live anywhere, at least according to my lawyer, but there was no erasing the news articles about the case.

Sometimes I regretted taking Kenny to court. I'd hoped to ruin his reputation in the same way he'd ruined mine, and I'd also hoped he would get some jail time. The bastard had more than deserved it.

But, unfortunately, disseminating intimate pictures online was only considered a misdemeanor in Connecticut, punishable by up to a year in jail.

Just a year. Unfuckingbelievable.

And the kicker in all this? The judge thought Kenny had "suffered enough" because he'd lost his job over the allegations of revenge porn and had decided not to sentence him to any time in prison.

Kenny still lived in our hometown and seemed to be doing just fine. He'd lost his job as a teacher, but he was now working for his uncle in construction.

Me? I hadn't been able to cope with the constant stares, snide remarks, and the fact that so many of my friends and family had turned their backs on me. Even my own parents.

The hurtful things both my family and friends had said to me in the aftermath of the pictures being posted rang in my head.

Disgusting! Why would you take a picture like that?

What were you thinking? Are you an idiot?

Do you have any idea how your sleazy behavior reflects on me and your mother?

Sorry, Gemma, I just don't want to be seen in public with you anymore.

Ten fucking naked pictures. In the course of my

two-year relationship with Kenny, I'd texted him ten naked pictures at his request. And the asshole had saved them all and decided to share them after our breakup. For no good reason, either, that I could tell. Just because he could. Just because he was a jerk. Just because he thought my daddy dom fantasies were "gross and unnatural" and I deserved to be publicly shamed in some way.

At least I hadn't married him. At least I hadn't told him about my needs after he'd given me his grandmother's ring and we'd exchanged vows. Bullet dodged there.

Should I assume that Derek/Daddy would Google my name? Maybe I should just confess my reasons for moving here before he found out on his own.

What if he saw the articles about the revenge porn case and thought badly of me? What if he thought I was stupid for having sent the pictures in the first place? That was a word many people had thrown in my face after the fact. Stupid.

I sighed and moved back to the window, wishing I could find the answer to my predicament in the gorgeous sunset.

This place is my fresh start.

Everything will work out. It must.

I hoped I wasn't lying to myself.

CHAPTER 16

DEREK

I rushed up the steps of Gemma's house and knocked on the door. It was just after nine in the morning, and I hoped she was awake. If she hadn't eaten yet, I planned to take her to breakfast again. In any case, I wanted to spend more time with her today. Maybe I could help her start getting her art studio set up. Didn't matter what we did, I just wanted to be in her presence. Her inherent sweetness and innocence shined light on the dark loneliness that had been my life for far too long.

It was time for a new beginning. Time to take a chance on love again.

Yes, I knew the average person would worry I was looney for thinking about love so soon in a relationship. But I didn't give a damn. I was so fiercely drawn to Gemma that logic didn't matter.

I knew one thing for certain: I wanted to be her Daddy.

I wanted her as both my woman and my baby girl.

The sound of footsteps rushing down the stairs inside the house brought a smile to my face. Though my smile quickly faded, and I held my breath as I listened to make sure she didn't slip on the stairs. She shouldn't be running in the house like that.

When she flung the door open, her look of joy upon seeing me warmed my heart, despite my displeasure with her for running on the stairs.

"Baby girl," I said in a strict tone, "you should know better than to run on the stairs."

Her eyes widened and a blush stained her cheeks. "Um, what?" Her look of feigned innocence made my cock go instantly hard.

Jesus. If we were going to keep spending time together, I might have to buy some jeans with a little more room in the crotch.

"Don't play innocent with me, young lady. I heard you running in the house." I lifted one eyebrow at her and gave her my best scowl. It was the sort of stern look that would make my ranch hands quake in their boots.

"Oops. Sorry, Daddy. I was just so excited to see you today." She flushed and laced her arms around my neck.

"Promise you won't do it again," I said.

"Okay, okay, I promise." She drew in a shaky breath. "I'm glad you stopped by. I was hoping you would." She smiled again, clearly happy to see me. Her joy was my joy.

I embraced her and lifted her up as I entered the door. I'd missed her and loved having her in my arms.

"Daddy! Put me down!" she said with a giggle.

I finally set her on her feet, though I kept my arms around her. Likewise, her arms were wrapped around my neck. I leaned down to place a quick kiss to her lips and took a moment to savor her familiar scent. Lavender and vanilla.

Her hair was damp from a recent shower, though braided into pigtails, and she was wearing jeans with a yellow blouse and a matching cardigan. With her golden locks and the vibrant shade of her clothing, she looked like pure sunshine. Felt like it, too. I hugged her tighter.

"You look cute today, Daddy," she said with a wide grin. I was just wearing my normal clothes—jeans, a flannel shirt, and my hat—but her praise brought a flush to my face, nonetheless.

"Thanks, baby girl. You're pretty cute yourself." I glanced over my shoulder. The door was still open, and a few tourists were bustling by. "Are you hungry?" I asked, looking back to her. "I'd love to take you out for pancakes again."

She beamed at me. "I'd like that, Daddy. Thank you." A sudden look of uncertainty came over her. "I-I was worried you wouldn't stop by today. After you rushed off last night."

I sighed. "I'm sorry about that, darlin'." I'd been in such a hurry to get back to the ranch last night that

I'd quickly told her I had a work emergency to deal with, gave her a good-bye kiss, and hurried back to the ranch. But now, I took the time to tell her about the resort guests who'd intentionally hiked a closed trail in hopes of catching sight of a bear.

Her eyes went wide. "Oh no! Did you find them? Please tell me they aren't still missing. Oh my... they didn't get devoured by a bear, did they?"

"Don't worry. No one got eaten by a bear. We found them. They'd wandered off the trail and gotten lost. They were dehydrated and hungry, but otherwise fine, and they never even made it close to the bears, thank goodness." I was still mentally and physically exhausted from yesterday's ordeal of rescuing the married couple who'd somehow thought it wouldn't be a big deal to hike down a closed path in search of bears, but I was glad all had ended well. After threatening the guests with permanent banishment from my resort, they'd apologized and promised to never break any of the rules again.

"Well, I'm glad to hear it," Gemma said. "Now, how about those pancakes you promised me?"

"I'm ready when you are, baby girl."

"Let me go grab my purse. Be right back." She turned and walked toward the stairs, and I was glad to see she was minding me, but then halfway up the steps, she broke into another run.

"Gemma! What did I just tell you? No running in the house!" I growled and walked toward the staircase.

She rushed down the steps with a wide grin

holding her purse, obviously not realizing how serious I was about this rule. But just as she reached me, her eyes widened, and she held up a finger. "I forgot my phone. Be right back, Daddy. Don't leave without me!"

She bolted upstairs before I could stop her. "Hey! Baby girl, you'd better slow down. No running on the stairs!"

By the time she rushed down the steps again, I was fuming. I grasped her arm and peered down at her, giving her a serious look. "Young lady, I'm not playing around. If I catch you running in the house one more time, you're going to regret it. No. Running. In. The. House. Understood?"

She lowered her head slightly. "Yes, Daddy," she said in an apologetic voice that sounded a bit forced to me, "I understand."

"Good. For your sake, I hope we don't have to revisit this topic." I guided her toward the door. "Now, I hope you're hungry for pancakes, baby girl, and I also hope you're in the mood to take a walk. It's a beautiful day."

GEMMA

I walked hand-in-hand with Daddy through town. Rather than take his truck to Kay's Diner, we'd decided to go on foot. I loved that he was giving me a personal tour of Rocky Springs. After we enjoyed a leisurely breakfast, he took me into several stores to introduce me to other business owners. Everyone I encountered gave me a warm welcome and a few even expressed interest in attending one of my paint nights.

When we finally arrived back at my brick rental, I was brimming with excitement and eager to finish setting up my art studio. I also needed to box up a few paintings I'd recently sold via my website and get them to the post office. Daddy pitched in to help and kept complimenting my artwork. His constant praise made me blush but also filled me with pride.

Back home, in Westport, I'd sold the same kind of abstract nature paintings in my gift shop, but more than a few people I'd gone to art school with had called me a sell-out for trying to cater to tourists.

You're mass-producing this stuff? You're actually hosting paint nights? Don't you ever want to make real art? You spent four years in art school and now you're doing this?

The snobbery was unreal. I'd heard it all, but I'd taken the criticism in stride because at least I was making a living doing something I loved. Sure, money was a bit tight while I waited for my shop in Connecticut to sell, but I was confident that things would turn around once my store in Rocky Springs was up and running. I'd done my research before moving here, and while I could've moved to a larger town that saw more tourists, the low cost of living in Rocky Springs made it the ideal place for me to move.

"Gemma, this place is looking fantastic." He

nodded toward the window that faced the street, where I'd placed a few larger paintings to help draw in customers. "I think if you put an open sign on the door right now, people would flood in."

I surveyed the studio with a critical eye just as a delivery truck rumbled to a stop in front of the building. Daddy was right. Maybe I could open early? The sound of footsteps on the porch drew my attention and I headed to the door to meet the delivery woman, who was holding a large box.

"Knock knock!" she said in a jovial tone.

"Hi, there. Thank you so much," I said, opening the screen door. But just before I could accept the box, Daddy swooped in front of me and took it.

"Good morning, Amy," Derek said with a friendly nod at the middle-aged woman with long dark hair. He tucked the huge box under one arm. "How've you been?"

The delivery woman—Amy—gave him a broad smile as she stood in the doorway. "Oh I've been all right. Just broke up with my boyfriend but damn if I don't feel two hundred pounds lighter now. What do you say, Derek? I'm currently conducting interviews for my next boy toy. Care to apply?" She winked at him, and I realized there was something very, very familiar about her. A second later, it hit me. She looked just like Kay from the diner. But in different clothes and with a different haircut.

Derek chuckled. "Amy, I'm touched that you would consider me, but I don't think I could handle you." He winked back at her, and another thought occurred to me. They looked to be around the same age. What if he liked her? What if he decided he would rather be with a woman closer to his own age?

Doubts and insecurities plagued me. I wanted a fresh start here, but I didn't want to begin my time in Rocky Springs with a broken heart. I stood awkwardly as I watched the interaction between Amy and Daddy continue to play out.

Amy chuckled and gave a wry shake of her head. "I'm just teasing, of course. From what I hear from Kay, you've already got yourself a woman." Her eyes drifted to me, and she gave me an appraising look. "You must be Gemma, the artist from Connecticut. Welcome to Rocky Springs! It's so nice to finally meet you. I'm Amy, of course." She offered me her hand and I promptly shook it. Her grip was firm, and she possessed a self-confidence I couldn't help but envy.

"Hi, Amy," I said. "It's so nice to meet you, too." Some of my insecurities from earlier started to fade. "Um, I hope this isn't a rude question, but are you Kay's sister?"

She smoothed a hand through her hair, then struck a dramatic pose as she cupped her own face. "Why yes, I am. I'm the younger, sexier twin. But don't tell Kay I said that or she'll put salt in my coffee!" She laughed and I found myself joining in. I also wished I could joke around and interact with people with as much ease as she could. She was the sort of person who was comfortable in her own skin. Oh how I wished I could be more like that.

We exchanged a few more pleasantries before she

finally announced she had to finish her route. She waved farewell and skipped down the porch steps to her waiting truck. I waved back, even though she no longer had her eyes on us. I shot an amused look at Daddy.

"She's a character," he said with a grin, "just like Kay."

"I think they're both very nice," I said, "though I'll admit I was worried for a second when she hit on you. I didn't realize she was joking at first." I didn't mention that her comment had also caused me to worry that maybe Daddy would decide he wanted to be with someone older than me, someone closer to his own age.

Daddy shut the screen door, set the box on the floor, then guided me into the center of the room. He wrapped his arms around me and kissed my forehead. The stubble on his face tickled my cheeks, and a spasm of heat rolled through my core. It seemed the smallest act of affection from him was enough to get my motor running.

"Baby girl," he said, playfully nuzzling his nose against mine, "even if she had been serious, you would've had nothing to worry about. I'm all yours, darlin', and you're all mine."

CHAPTER 17

GEMMA

I GASPED WITH DELIGHT WHEN I OPENED THE BOX and peered inside. More supplies for the giftshop side of my studio—the keychains, magnets, t-shirts, etcetera—had arrived. I was still expecting a few more boxes, but this was a great start.

"My tacky tourist doodads!" I said, pulling out a handful of keychains that were miniature depictions of my most popular abstract mountainous landscape painting.

Daddy knelt next to me on the floor and peered into the box. He pulled out a t-shirt that had a colorful rising sun on it, another of my most popular paintings. For these particular items, I'd decided to use the prints that frequently sold out on my website.

I giggled as he removed his flannel shirt followed by his navy-blue undershirt. And then my eyes promptly widened, and my throat went dry. Oh my. Daddy was ripped. His sculpted chest was spattered with dark hair, making him appear extra rugged and manly. My heart fluttered and warmth spasmed between my thighs. This was the first time I'd seen Daddy naked from the waist up.

He seemed oblivious to my gawking as he pulled the t-shirt he'd grabbed from the box over his head. He shoved his arms through the holes and tugged it down. Facing me, he placed his hands on his hips, modeling the shirt with a wide grin. He made a flourishing motion at the text that was printed below the sun: Gemma's Gallery, Rocky Springs, CO.

"Now I'm a walking advertisement for your studio." His warm smile nearly brought tears to my eyes. A couple of days ago, I hadn't even known he existed, but today his support meant the world to me.

"Thank you, Daddy." I rose to my feet and looked him up and down. "You look very nice in that shirt, but... you also looked pretty nice without a shirt at all." My face promptly grew hot.

Before he could respond, I heard my cell phone ringing. All the way upstairs. Crap. I'd left it on the kitchen counter.

"I'll be right back!" I called as I bolted toward the stairs.

"No running, baby girl," Daddy said. "Not in the house and most certainly not on the stairs."

With a dramatic sigh, I slowed my pace, but only to a slow jog. I didn't want to miss the call. What if it was the sign people saying they could come early? Or what if my accountant needed to reach me? I realized if it was important, whoever was calling would likely leave a message, but I didn't want to take the chance. Especially when cell phone service could be spotty in Rocky Springs. As I reached the kitchen, I made a mental note to have a landline installed as soon as possible.

"Hello?" I said after swiping the answer button. I moved my mouth away from the phone a second later so the person on the other end wouldn't hear my heavy breathing.

"Hello, we've been trying to reach you about your car's extended warranty..." came a robotic female voice.

I moved the phone away from my ear, glared at the screen, and said, "Oh, go fuck yourself, Robot Lady." I ended the call and returned my phone to the counter.

When I spun around, I gasped at the sight of Daddy standing in the doorway with his arms crossed over his broad chest. He'd put the flannel shirt on over the sun t-shirt, but he'd left it unbuttoned so you could still see the front. His face was set in stern lines that sent a quiver across my butt cheeks.

"Young lady," he said in a scolding voice, "I thought I told you not to run on the stairs." He lifted one dark eyebrow at me, causing nerves to flutter in my tummy.

Uh oh. Daddy didn't look happy at all.

"Um, well, I slowed down a little bit, Daddy," I said, wondering if I would be able to talk my way out of trouble. Would he spank me for disobeying him? I supposed I was about to find out. Heat quaked in my nether region at the thought of getting a spanking from Daddy.

"You barely slowed down, baby girl. That staircase is steep and doesn't have any carpeting or slip-resistant strips on it. And you're just wearing socks right now. You could've easily slipped and hurt yourself." A vein in his temple pulsed and I suddenly realized this wasn't for play. Daddy was upset with me for real. In all fairness, he *had* warned me a couple of times today not to run in the house and especially not on the stairs.

"Sorry, Daddy," I said. "I promise I won't do it again."

"I've half a mind to punish you for the bad language I just heard you use as well, but I have never given you explicit orders not to cuss, so I suppose that wouldn't be fair. But hear me out now, young lady. If I hear that kind of vulgarity escaping your lips again, I will wash your mouth out with soap *and* redden your bottom." He cleared his throat, dropped his arms to his sides, and approached me. I was already leaning against the kitchen counter, so when he reached me, I was trapped. "But I *have* explicitly told you not to run in the house multiple times now, haven't I?"

Yikes. I knew where he was going with this, and now I was getting worried I really wouldn't be able to talk my way out of a punishment. "Um, I guess you have warned me a few times not to run in the house. I'm sorry, Daddy, and it absolutely positively one hundred percent won't happen again. Never ever ever." I flashed him a polite smile and hoped he believed me.

The idea of getting in trouble with Daddy was both exciting but also scary. Exciting because it was real, and scary because I had a feeling this spanking might hurt considerably more than the first two spankings he'd given me. The spankings that had been more role play than anything.

"I have warned you exactly four times, Gemma, not to run in the house," he said, taking my chin between his fingers as he forced me to meet his stern gaze, "yet you keep disobeying." He was quiet for a long, tense moment. "I think you know what happens to disobedient little girls who risk their safety."

"I, um..." My voice trailed off and I grasped for something intelligible to say. Perhaps I ought to accept the fact that I had a real punishment spanking coming. Perhaps if I was truly repentant and cooperative, Daddy might not go so hard on me. Another tingle raced across my ass.

He stepped closer, allowing me to feel the heat of his huge body. Leaning down to place his lips at my ear, he said, "I know a little girl who's about to get a spanking from her Daddy."

CHAPTER 18

DEREK

I PLANNED TO INSTALL SOME SLIP RESISTANT STRIPS on the stairs very soon. But even so, I didn't want Gemma constantly running up and down the steep staircase. She was a big girl and ought to know better. Never mind the fact that I'd warned her numerous times not to run in the house and especially not on the stairs.

I didn't like the idea of her getting hurt, and it displeased me that she wasn't taking her well-being very seriously. What if she fell down the steps when I wasn't here and really hurt herself? That thought alone was enough to convince me that I needed to be firm with her. A verbal warning or a time-out wouldn't suffice.

She needed a spanking. A hard one. On her bare little bottom.

I released her chin and turned to grab a kitchen chair. I pulled the chair into the center of the room, just as I had yesterday. But that spanking hadn't been a true punishment, and she was about to discover just how easy I'd gone on her during that flirting/role play session.

I rolled up my sleeves and then sank down on the chair. With my gaze steady on her, I patted my thigh and gave her an expectant look. "Come here, naughty girl. Come to Daddy."

She approached me with slow steps but finally reached my side. She bowed her head and started fidgeting in place. Her obvious nervousness made my cock harden and my balls draw up tight.

As she chewed on her bottom lip, she reached around to cup her backside. "Please, Daddy," she said in a pleading tone that sent more blood rushing to my manhood. "Please don't spank me too hard. I really am sorry." Her voice was quiet and small, and she sounded truly sorry, but that wouldn't change things. I had to make sure she didn't risk her safety again.

I drew her to stand between my spread legs. Even with me sitting and her standing, she wasn't much taller than me. The urge to wrap my arms around her and protect her swept through me, an intense need that stole my breath.

With deft movements, I unfastened the front of her jeans, though I didn't pull them down yet. Her hands trembled at her sides, and she kept chewing on her bottom lip. There was also an increasingly worried gleam in her pretty dark eyes.

"You're extra adorable when you're repentant and nervous, baby girl, however, that won't save you from the firm spanking you have coming. Daddy needs to teach you a lesson, doesn't he?"

She nodded. "Yes, Daddy, I suppose so."

"Tell me why you're about to get a spanking on your bare bottom, young lady. I want to hear you say it." I leaned back and watched her, ready to make a grab for her if she tried to bolt. More than once since she'd come to stand in front of me, she'd looked over her shoulder at the doorway.

"I'm gettin' a spankin' 'cause I was naughty and ran in the house and ran on the stairs even though Daddy said not to." She spoke quickly but quietly, in a voice so low I almost couldn't make out her words. "And I guess that's dangerous, and I'm not supposed to do it."

"That's right, baby girl. You did something dangerous even after Daddy warned you not to and you put yourself at risk of getting hurt. Daddy doesn't want to see you hurt. I want to keep you safe, Gemma. Always. And that's why I'm going to punish you right now. It's my hope that after I finish reddening your naughty little bottom, you'll think twice about putting yourself in danger again."

She gave a slight nod, then glanced over her shoulder at the doorway once more. I hoped she wasn't foolish enough to try bolting. I'd catch her immediately and she would be lucky if she sat comfortably for the next week if she pulled a stunt like that. Fortunately, she turned to face me again, swallowing hard as her gaze danced to mine briefly before she peered at a random spot on the wall behind me. Her face was dark pink, evidence of her deep shame.

"All right, let's get these jeans off of you, young lady." I pulled her pants down and helped her step out of them, though I left her panties on. I would pull those down once she was over my lap. I patted my thigh and gave her an expectant look. "Time to go over Daddy's knee."

Anxiety flashed across her face, though she was quick to obey my command. She placed herself over my left knee, and once she was settled in position with her bottom lifted high, I draped my right leg over hers. I planned to give her a hard spanking and I didn't want her trying to escape my lap once her punishment began.

I cupped her bottom overtop her panties, massaging gently. She shivered and took a deep breath while I continued rubbing her ass. Finally, once I sensed her beginning to relax, I pulled her panties down to her knees. I also reached for her hands and pinned them at the small of her back.

"This is going to be fast and hard, baby girl, and I don't want to risk your hands getting hurt if you reach back to shield your bottom," I explained.

"Okay, Daddy," she murmured, and her body tensed, as though she expected the first smack to fall at any moment.

I didn't make her wait long. I lifted my hand and brought my palm down sharply upon her ass, spanking her hard and fast, just as I'd promised. I aimed most of the blows to the center of her cheeks, though I occasionally swatted her lower, on her sit-spot and even on the back of her upper thighs.

"Oh! Owie, owie, owwwww, Daddy!" She cried out and writhed over my lap as I rained down smack after smack.

"This is what happens to naughty baby girls who disobey their daddies," I scolded. "This is what happens when you risk your safety, young lady."

As I spanked her, her thighs widened during her struggles, revealing the sweetness within. So pink and gleaming and swollen. Even though this was a real punishment spanking, she was quickly becoming soaking wet. Eventually, once I'd administered about two dozen smacks, her engorged clit poked out from her slick folds. God, I couldn't wait to touch her, to stroke her privates and bring her pleasure.

But there would be no pleasure until she'd learned her lesson. Until she was red-bottomed and thoroughly punished. Until she was one very sorry little girl.

I gave her a few more smacks before stopping. Her shoulders were heaving slightly, and I could hear her sniffling. My heart clenched when I realized I'd spanked her to tears, though I reminded myself that this was necessary. If I didn't put a stop to her constant running—in socks in a house with nothing but hardwood floors throughout—it was only a matter of time before she had an accident and got hurt.

Her punished flesh was warm under my hand as I

went back to massaging her cheeks, this time on her bare bottom.

"Shh, sweet girl, it's over now." I gently lifted her up and got her situated on my lap. As I wiped at her tear-stained face, she avoided meeting my gaze. Eventually, I lifted her chin and stared directly into her eyes. "It's over now," I repeated, "and you took your spanking well. I'm proud of you, little one."

The mixture of relief and gratitude that suddenly filled her eyes took me aback. I froze as I stared at her. She was looking at me the same way Trisha used to after being punished. Relieved it was over, but also thankful that she had someone to hold her accountable for her behavior. My throat closed up and my chest tightened, though not from despair or regret. Instead, I found myself in awe of the situation as I too experienced feelings of immense gratitude.

Because finally, finally, after too many years of painful solitude, I had a sweet baby girl to call my own.

I would never forget Trisha, and I wasn't trying to replace her with Gemma. I would love my late wife forever, but that didn't mean there wasn't room in my heart for the young lady in my arms.

A second chance at love.

A second chance at being a daddy.

It was almost too good to be true.

I tightened my arms around Gemma and buried my face in her lavender-vanilla scented hair.

<h1 style="text-align:center">CHAPTER 19</h1>

GEMMA

Well, my butt hurt. I rolled over in bed and sighed. Then I rubbed my bottom over my drop-seat jammies. Daddy had given me a firm spanking yesterday. Ouch.

But my thoughts soon strayed to what had happened after my punishment. He'd held me. For a long time. He'd whispered soothing phrases into my ear, told me he cared about me, and kept kissing my forehead. He'd also wiped away my tears and repeatedly asked if I was all right.

I liked that he'd taken care of me after spanking me, though I was still incredibly embarrassed that I'd been naughty enough to warrant a punishment in the first place. And all because of a car warranty robocall...

I sat up against the pillows and hugged Mr. Rabbit

to my chest as I remembered how sweetly Daddy had carried me to my bed after we had a cuddle. He'd placed me under the covers and sat on the edge of my bed while giving me a sexy, heated look. Then he'd asked if I wanted *special rubs* between my legs.

Even now, heat gathered in my core and a steady pulse built as I recalled how expertly he'd brought me to a release, and only using his fingers. But I resisted the urge to touch myself. Not because I worried Daddy might find out, but because I had a schedule to keep today.

I glanced at the clock on the nightstand and groaned. Better get a move on. I hopped out of bed, leaving Mr. Rabbit behind, and hurried for the shower. A fast walk—not a run or even a slow jog. Nope, I'd learned my lesson.

After I showered and dressed, I made a quick breakfast and then headed downstairs to my art studio. A few custom orders had come in on my website last night and I planned to spend the morning working on them.

Around noon, the sign people were stopping by to take measurements, and Daddy would be here around one thirty with a late lunch. He had a staff meeting this morning at his ranch resort that couldn't be missed.

I put on some music and started to get organized in my studio when my phone buzzed in my pocket. It was a Connecticut number that I didn't recognize, but I decided to answer anyway, on the off chance it was my accountant or lawyer calling from a new number.

Or maybe it was the realtor calling with good news about the building I was selling in Westport. It would be fabulous if someone had made an offer on my former studio.

"Hello?" I said.

"Little baby Gemma," came a familiar, snide voice.

Coldness gripped me. "What the hell do you want? And how'd you get this number?"

"I'll tell you what I want. Fifty fucking thousand dollars, that's what I want."

Money. Of course, this was about money. "I don't even have the full fifty thousand, you idiot. It's being garnished from your wages. I get a small amount each month deposited into my account, numb nuts." Oh it felt good to call him names. What was he going to do? Fly two thousand miles so he could insult me to my face?

"I know you don't have it all yet, bitch." The raw anger in his tone came as a shock. He'd always been an asshole, but he'd never spoken to me with such venom in his voice before. "But eventually, you'll have the full fifty thousand, so I figure you ought to give it to me all now to save me the trouble of getting it from you later. It's my money, not yours. I don't give a fuck what the judge says. You have no right to it."

"Because of you, because of what you did, I had to move. I had to close my studio in Westport and move far away. Do you have any idea how expensive moving is?" I gripped my phone harder. "You fucked up my whole life, and for what? Why? Just because we broke up?"

"Yes!" he roared, "because we broke up! It was just a little fight, it wasn't supposed to be permanent. And the following week, after our fight, when I told you I wanted to get back together, you refused. You fucking refused. You of all people. A disgusting pervert. You think you can be picky?" He scoffed and I thought I heard him take a swig of something. Drunk. Of course. I should've figured.

"As I've explained to you many times before, I didn't refuse to get back together with you just to be mean, Kenny. I refused because I knew we weren't compatible. You could've walked away peacefully and left me alone and everything would've been fine. But what did you do? You threatened to make me sorry, and then a few days later, I found out you shared intimate pictures of me online. You hurt me and you broke my trust in the worst way possible, and you showed me your true colors in the process. You're an awful person and I want nothing to do with you, and if you think for one second I might give you any of that money you think you're entitled to, you're a fucking idiot." My voice shook with rage, and I wiped away a fallen tear. I couldn't believe he'd called me. Only a handful of people had this number.

"I know where you are, bitch," he said, and my stomach clenched with fear.

"Congrats on knowing how to use the goddamn internet," I said, figuring he'd searched the new address for my art studio. I'd known it wouldn't be impossible for people from my former life to find me, but I'd come all the way to Rocky Springs hoping that no one would bother looking. I didn't want to be found. Especially not by a jizz rag like Kenny.

"I know where you are and if you don't arrange to start giving me back some of my money soon, I'll make you sorry. One way or another, I'll make you pay." The line went dead, and I stared at my phone in disbelief.

I sighed and ran a hand through my hair. I needed to call my lawyer and let her know about Kenny's threats. I hoped he wouldn't try to share pictures of me on the internet again. Investigators had promised the photos had been wiped clean from his hard drive and from his phone. But that didn't mean he didn't have a secret backup somewhere. Hell, he could've printed out the photos and hidden them under his freaking mattress for all I knew. Wouldn't put it past the degenerate fuckface.

A sinking feeling came over me. Someone had given Kenny my new cell phone number. But who? Three friends from Westport, my parents, my lawyer, my realtor, and my accountant. No one else had my new number. My parents still weren't speaking to me —but I'd texted them the number a few weeks ago. Just in case of an emergency.

I called my lawyer but groaned when I got her answering machine. Nevertheless, I left a detailed message telling her about my conversation with Kenny. After that, I set my phone aside and took a few deep breaths.

A spell of dizziness threatened to send me to the floor, and I gripped the edges of my chair so I wouldn't take a tumble. Not that I'd ever fainted or even fallen during one of my nervous dizzy spells before. But I still felt like I needed to hold onto something, just in case.

Tears blurred my vision, and I blinked rapidly as I swallowed past the burning in my throat. I wouldn't cry because of Kenny. I wouldn't. Never again.

A few minutes later, the dizziness had passed, and I no longer felt on the verge of tears. I turned the music back up, faced the blank canvas, and picked up a paintbrush. Until the doorbell rang a few hours later, announcing the arrival of the sign company, I threw myself into my work and channeled my emotions onto the canvas.

CHAPTER 20

DEREK

WHEN I ARRIVED AT GEMMA'S, I SMILED AS I noticed the temporary vinyl banner that was hanging on the front porch. *Gemma's Gallery*. Holding the bag that contained our lunch under one arm, I rushed up the steps and rang the doorbell. A few seconds later, Gemma appeared at the door wearing a paint covered apron. There were also streaks of paint on her arms, face, and neck. My heart swelled at the sight of her.

"Hey, Daddy!" A smile lit up her face.

"Good afternoon, sweetheart," I said, leaning down to kiss her cheek. "I hope you're hungry."

"I'm famished," she said. "Come on in." She backed up and opened the door wider to permit my entry.

Her studio looked even better than it had when I'd left last night. She'd put a few more paintings on display, and she'd also organized the "doodads" she planned to sell into colorful bins. There were also two hanging racks of t-shirts near the counter that I imagined would be the checkout area.

"Wow, Gemma, you've been busy. I hope you didn't stay up all night doing this. If I'd known you planned to work more after I left yesterday, I would've stayed longer."

She aimed a guilty smile in my direction, and I noticed her eyes looked both tired and happy. "I was too excited about possibly opening the studio sooner than planned that I couldn't sleep, so I figured I'd get some work done." She covered a sudden yawn and then emitted a soft chuckle.

"Looks like you've been painting, too." I peered around her studio. There were dozens of completed paintings that were already framed and appeared ready for sale, but I spotted several easels set up in a corner of the shop that held half-finished works.

She nodded and wiped at a smudge of paint on her face. "I had a few custom orders come in recently, and I figured I'd get a start on those as well." She looked at the bag I was holding. "Thanks for bringing lunch, Daddy. I'm starving."

We went upstairs and I unpacked our lunch while she washed up. Or tried to. Not all the paint was coming off her arms or her face. Once she got her hands clean, she joined me at the table.

"This looks delicious," she said, eyeing the cheeseburger and fries on her plate.

We both dug into our meals with gusto and ate in

silence for a few minutes. But it wasn't an awkward silence. I enjoyed her company, and I very much hoped that she enjoyed mine. I was about to make a comment about how she needed a bath—and suggest that I help clean her—when it struck me that we still knew so very little about one another. We'd spent a great deal of time together these past few days, yet most of that time had been spent flirting, kissing, and... spanking.

I drew in a deep breath and peered into her pretty dark eyes. I ought to tell her more about myself. I ought to be honest with her. Everyone knew everyone in Rocky Springs, and it wouldn't be long before someone mentioned to her that I was a widower. I would tell her. Soon. But first, I wanted to learn more about Gemma and her past. Like the reason she'd left Connecticut all on her own and moved about two thousand miles from home to open up a business. People didn't just up and move away from their home-town for no good reason. Had she left because of the bad breakup with the asshole who'd called her disgust-ing? Or had something else happened? A hundred different scenarios rushed through my mind and my curiosity about her grew.

"So, did you have an art studio back in Connecti-cut?" I asked, trying to keep my tone casual.

A shadow crossed her face, but she soon smiled. A forced smile. One that didn't reach her eyes. "Yes, I had a shop in Westport, where I'm from. Opened it just after I graduated from art school." A wistful look came over her. "My grandfather bought me the building as a graduation present. He died not long after that, but he got to see the grand opening of my studio. It's one of my favorite memories. He was always one of my biggest champions. My parents thought art school would be a waste of time and money—not that it was even their money, I took out student loans—and they kept trying to dissuade me from going. But my grandfather was always so encouraging."

"I'm sorry to hear about your grandfather's passing," I said. "Sounds like you two were close."

She nodded. "I spent more time at his house than at my parents' growing up. I miss him. But he lived a long and happy life. He played in a local band and used to take me to his shows. And he always made sure I had plenty of painting supplies at his house, since my mother didn't like the mess and claimed we didn't have enough space for it."

I was happy to learn she'd had a loving grandfather who'd helped to raise her, someone who'd encouraged her to follow her dreams, but it also saddened me to learn her parents had been dismissive and perhaps even distant. "Do you have a better relationship with your parents these days? Now that they can see for themselves that you're successful and brilliant at what you do?"

She blushed when I said "brilliant," though she soon appeared hesitant to answer. She avoided my gaze and swallowed hard. Finally, she lifted her eyes to mine. "Actually, I don't really talk to my parents anymore. They don't want much to do with me. They were angry that my grandfather spent all his money on me. When he died, he didn't have much to pass on to my mom. She'd been counting on that money and blamed me for it. She'd had plans to retire early, along with my dad, and buy a vacation house in Maine and was pissed that she could no longer do that. I ruined their retirement plans." She bit her lower lip and her gaze fell to the table.

"Hey," I said in a gentle voice as I reached for her hand. I entwined my fingers with hers and squeezed. "You didn't ruin anything. Your grandfather had every right to do what he wanted with his money, and I think he made a good choice. Besides, I bet you made his final years special. It sounds like the two of you spent a lot of time together. I'm sure he loved you very, very much."

CHAPTER 21

GEMMA

I blinked back tears and felt like a liar. Not because I'd told a fib to Daddy, but because I wasn't telling him the full truth. It was a fact that my parents weren't happy my grandfather had bought me the building in Westport. And it was true that the money he'd spent on me had caused a rift in our family, but the real reason I'd left Westport had little to do with my parents.

Kenny. The intimate pictures. The shame and the gossip. I'd fled my hometown because of my hateful ex and the embarrassment he'd caused me. How could I remain in a town where almost everyone looked at me as though I were a whore, a pervert, stupid, or all of the above? Thank God he hadn't told anyone (that I knew of) about my interest in the daddy dom/little girl lifestyle. He'd called me disgusting in private, but in public, he'd only shared the nude pictures of me. Small mercies, I suppose.

"Are you okay?" Daddy asked, a concerned gleam in his eyes. "I'm sorry I brought up a painful memory for you. That wasn't my intention. I simply wished to understand you better. This might sound corny, but in some ways I feel like I've known you my whole life, Gemma, but in other ways, you're a stranger to me." The comforting smile he shot me was like a warm hug.

"I'm okay." I sighed, wishing I could tell him everything. But what if he rejected me? What if he judged me the way so many others had? I didn't know if I would be able to withstand Daddy's condemnation. I was really starting to like him, starting to believe that we might be able to enjoy a long-term relationship.

It was bad enough that Kenny had my number. Bad enough that he'd called me this morning. I was still reeling from the shock of hearing his voice on the phone, and it unnerved me that he thought I owed him money. Especially when thus far, I'd only received about six thousand of the fifty thousand he'd been ordered to pay me.

I stared across the table at Daddy, feeling vulnerable and worried. He hadn't been in my life for very long, but I didn't want to lose him. He'd been so kind to me so far, and he'd allowed me to safely start exploring my little side with him.

But I wasn't the only one with secrets. He still hadn't told me about his late wife. Was he ever planning to tell me? Or was it a private pain he wished to hold close to his heart forever?

"I'm glad I met you, Gemma," he said, holding my hand tighter. His eyes beamed with so much affection, my throat started to burn. "You're a remarkable woman and a sweet little girl. You're brave, too. Pardon my language, but it takes serious balls to move across the country and start over like you're doing. I'm proud of you."

Despite the emotion constricting my throat, I had the abrupt urge to dance around the kitchen. Proud. Daddy was proud of me. And it wasn't the first time he'd told me that either.

"Thanks for saying that, Daddy. I-I hope I can make a real home for myself here in Rocky Springs. I did a lot of research when I was trying to decide where to move, and, well, I kept coming back to this town. Beyond the low cost of living and the growing tourism industry, I just had a feeling." It was true. I'd had a feeling. The first time I'd glimpsed photos of the town and the surrounding countryside, the beautiful snow-capped mountains and the gorgeous wildflowers that grew in springtime and early summer, I'd known this was the place for me.

"I have a feeling you'll be making a permanent home here." He drew in a long breath. "And maybe one day we'll even make a home together." He paled a bit after he said this, and his eyes widened too, as though he couldn't quite believe what he'd just said. I couldn't quite believe it either. Holy crap on a saltine cracker.

I didn't know what to say.

Daddy released my hand and looked extremely uncomfortable. Flustered. Embarrassed, even. Wanting to reassure him that I wasn't rejecting him, I stood up and walked around the table to him. Then I crawled right into his lap and laced my arms around his neck. I pressed a kiss to his forehead the way he always did for me, and when I pulled back, I was delighted to see a smile tugging at his lips.

"I would be lying if I said I haven't been imagining what it might be like if we lived together, Daddy. I had the balls to move away from my hometown and start over, but I guess I didn't have the balls to tell you that until just now." I giggled at the shocked look that crossed his face. "Pardon my language," I added. "So, what I'm trying to say is, don't be embarrassed by what you just said, Daddy, because I'm thinking the same thing. I'm also thinking, 'holy crap, things are moving really fast and oh my gosh what if we are making a mistake?' but other than that we're on the same page."

He wrapped his arms around me and pressed a firm kiss to my lips. Heat pulsed in my core, and I shifted on his lap until I felt the hard bulge of his erection beneath me. Oh yes. Daddy was getting excited. My breath hitched as a sexy growl rumbled from his throat.

Was it weird that we'd talked about moving in together before we'd even had sex? I wasn't certain, but I was certain about one thing: I really wanted Daddy to spend the night tonight. I wanted us to do grown-up things. My pulse spiked at the thought of us finally joining our bodies as one. Would Daddy be gentle or rough in the bedroom? I really wanted to find out.

He studied my face before looking at my paint-covered arms. "Baby girl, you're in dire need of a bath, don't you think?"

I glanced down at myself before meeting his eyes again. Warm pulses quickened between my thighs as I wondered what it would be like if Daddy gave me a bath. Is that what he meant? Or did he mean for me to clean up on my own? I gnawed on my lower lip, unsure of how to respond. Eventually, I said, "Yes, Daddy, I'm very dirty. I should probably take a bath."

His nostrils flared and I could've sworn his cock throbbed larger and harder beneath my bottom. "Would you like Daddy to help you, baby girl? Would you like Daddy to give you a thorough bath and help get you all clean?"

"Yes, Daddy, please," I gasped out, breathless with anticipation. A bath. Daddy wanted to give me a bath. A very intimate yet loving activity between a daddy and his baby girl. We hadn't even had sex yet, but this was almost as good.

He pushed the chair back, lifted me in his arms, and headed for the master bathroom.

CHAPTER 22

DEREK

DESIRE PUMMELED THROUGH ME AS I CARRIED
Gemma to the bathroom. I set her down in front of
the clawfoot tub and gazed at her. "Daddy's going to
get you nice and clean, baby girl. Then I'm going to
put you in a pair of cute jammies and you're going to
take a nap."

Her eyes widened with outrage. "A nap? But
Daddy! I don't need a nap. I'm not tired. I'm not."

I aimed her a stern look. "Yes, a nap. No argu-
ments, baby girl, or I'll redden your bottom. Is that
what you want? To be put down for your nap with a
sore butt?"

She released a shuddering breath. "No, Daddy, I
don't want a spanking. But I don't want a nap either."
She appeared suddenly sad. "I-I was hoping we could

spend the whole day together. If I'm sleeping, that takes away from our time together."

I thought of the overnight bag I'd left in my truck. I'd packed it *just in case*, though I hadn't carried it inside yet, as I hadn't wanted to appear presumptuous. Would she be amenable to me spending the night? I cleared my throat. "How about this, little Gemma? If you take a nice long nap, Daddy will stay the night."

Her face lit up like the sun. "Oh! Daddy, that's the best plan I've ever heard. It's a deal!" She sucked in a quick breath. "Um, Daddy, can I ask a question?"

"Anything. What is it?"

"Since you're spending the night, does that mean we're going to have, um, *grown-up fun?*" She stepped close enough that her lower stomach pressed against my throbbing hard cock.

I reached between her thighs and groped her pussy overtop her jeans, wishing she'd worn a dress or a skirt today. She looked adorable in jeans, but I preferred having easy access to her bottom and the sweetness between her thighs. "That depends on how achy and wet your privates become, baby girl. Do you think you're going to get wet and swollen for Daddy?"

A whimper escaped her, and desire flared in her gaze. "I'm already achy and wet for you, Daddy."

I pressed my hand harder to her crotch and she undulated against my touch with a needy moan. "Well, in that case, I suppose we ought to get you out of these jeans and your panties before you make a mess." I withdrew my hand from between her thighs and unfastened her pants. "How about Daddy checks to see just how wet you are? It sounds like you're going to need a thorough cleansing in the tub before your nap."

Her eyes became hooded with passion. "But I thought you wanted me wet and achy for our, um, grown-up activities?" Her lips parted and she inhaled deeply before adding, "Maybe we could have grown-up fun before my nap?"

I opened my mouth, preparing to tell her that she was taking a nap immediately after her bath and that was final, but my pants were getting so tight, it was becoming difficult to think straight. "We'll see, baby girl, we'll see. First, you need a bath." I proceeded to push her pants and panties down together and helped her step out of them. I picked up the clothing and set her jeans on a nearby chair, neatly folded. But I held onto her panties and inspected the large wet spot in the crotch. I held them up and pointed at the wet spot. "Look at this, baby girl. Look at the mess you made in your panties. I bet your pussy lips are soaking wet, too."

"Daddy, you're embarrassing me." She blushed and took a step back.

"There's nothing to be ashamed about," I said. "Sometimes little girls get wet and achy between their thighs, and it's a daddy's job to help them feel better. It's a daddy's job to help make the aching go away."

She eyed her panties dubiously before nodding. "Okay, Daddy, if you say so."

I placed her panties atop her folded jeans and eyed

the smooth bare folds of her pussy. My gaze traveled up to her shirt, which was tented by her hardened nipples. Jesus. She wasn't wearing a bra today.

I stepped closer to her. "Let's get this shirt off you. Lift your arms, please." Once she obeyed, I gently pulled the shirt over her head. A moment later, all the breath left my lungs. No bra. Just as I'd suspected. "You're beautiful, baby girl. So beautiful." My fingers tingled to touch her breasts, to trace her peaked nipples, but I needed to get the bath started. If I began pawing at her, we might end up doing grown-up things right here on the bathroom floor.

"Thank you, Daddy," she murmured, blushing yet again.

I got the bath running and added some bubbles. When I noticed a few rubber duckies sitting nearby, I added those to the water too. I turned to Gemma. "Come here, sweet girl, and let Daddy see just how wet your privates are."

Her eyes widened, but she soon complied, walking over to me and coming to a stop in front of the tub. She glanced at the water and the floating ducks, then peered at the bulge in my jeans. I didn't bother trying to hide my desire for her. I was half-tempted to shuck my own pants just to get some much-needed relief. But I decided to keep my clothes on. For now. I wanted to ease her into our first night together without scaring her. We were already moving at light speed.

"Move your feet apart, sweetheart. Spread your legs for Daddy."

She inhaled a shaky breath but was quick to obey. Once her legs were spread, I reached out and ran one finger along the seam of her pussy lips. Soaking wet. Just as I'd suspected. There was a definite glimmer on her thighs as well.

My little girl was so aroused that her essence had slipped out to trickle down her inner thighs. My cock thickened in my pants and my balls tightened with desire. I knelt before her to better inspect her swollen pussy.

God how I ached to thrust my shaft deep into her sweetness and spill myself inside her.

"Good girl," I said in a praising tone. "Daddy likes it when you listen."

She flushed and whimpered as I delved my finger into her hot, wet core to caress her slick inner folds. I added another finger and coated my digits in her essence, then dragged her arousal onto her inner thighs, adding to the glimmer that was already there. The scent of her excitement drove me wild. I longed to taste her and feel her shatter on my tongue as I lapped at her engorged clit.

"Look at all this wetness," I said, gesturing at her inner thighs. I rose to my feet and reached for her elbow. "Time to get you in the water, baby girl. You need a long, thorough bath. And considering how wet you are between your legs, Daddy's going to have to spend extra time cleaning your privates."

CHAPTER 23

GEMMA

A bath. A bath! Daddy was giving me a bath. I could scarcely believe it. I was also so turned on that I was pretty sure I would come the moment he next dragged a finger across my clit. I hoped that would be soon.

When he'd touched my pussy a moment ago, he'd avoided caressing my swollen nubbin. Instead, he'd focused on the moisture from my inner core, focused on dragging it out onto my thighs, as though to demonstrate just how incredibly wet I'd become.

He helped me into the water just as the bubbles reached the top of the tub. He got me settled and then turned the knob, shutting off the flow of water. I sighed with contentment at the warmth that surrounded me and soothed my aching muscles. Unpacking and getting my studio ready had taken its toll on my body. I was in pretty good shape, but I wasn't used to hard manual labor.

Daddy reached for a washcloth and dipped it into the water before rubbing a bar of soap on it and working up a lather. His eyes darkened with lust as he glanced at my breasts, and I resisted the urge to sink fully into the water.

He'd already seen me completely naked, and I'd gotten the sense that he'd liked what he saw. I wanted him to spend the night and claim me, and I supposed the best way to ensure that happened was to keep tempting him. Which meant not shyly covering my nudity, even if it was mildly shocking to have a man I'd met only days ago staring at my breasts.

A look of concentration filled his eyes as he started cleaning me, running the soapy cloth up and down each of my arms, removing the paint. He dabbed the cloth to several spots on my face next, as well as my neck. I'd fallen into the creative flow of my work deeper than usual today and hadn't paid any attention to dripping or smudged paint. I'd only cared about the story on the canvas I was trying to tell, because when I was telling a story through my painting, it distracted me from my worries.

"There you go," Daddy said in a warm tone. "All the paint is gone now. But you aren't completely clean yet. Get on your hands and knees and lift your bottom out of the water so I can better access your privates, baby girl."

My face flamed, though I did as he asked. He assisted me in getting into position and urged my butt higher in the air. I felt the water cascade down my bottom and upper thighs as I arched this part of my body out of the bath. He cupped my wet ass and gave it a firm squeeze, a growl of approval rumbling from deep in his chest.

"You look so adorable right now, Gemma," he said, "with your bottom lifted out of the water, your butt cheeks and the folds between your thighs all soapy and wet." He spent a long time running the cloth over the curve of my bottom. I trembled with desire and struggled to remain in place with my ass lifted to his liking.

He hummed as he cleaned me, though he hadn't actually started cleaning my pussy or between my checks yet. I flushed as the anticipation built. A whimper left me when the aching in my core became too much. I was seriously considering reaching between my thighs to stroke myself. My need was that great. I was burning up and restless, my heart pounding against my ribcage and my blood heating with each rapid breath.

"Please, Daddy," I said, not above begging. "Please, I can't take the aching anymore. Could you please help me?"

"Hm. Is it really that bad?"

I resisted the urge to huff. "Yes, Daddy. I can barely stand it. I-I need you to touch me. Down there."

He set the cloth aside and sat on the edge of the tub. Then he grabbed hold of my cheeks and spread my bottom wide. Oh God. Oh no. I couldn't believe what he was doing. I tried to fall out of position, but he made a stern tsking noise that encouraged me to get back in place.

"Settle down, little one, or Daddy will have to spank you. Is that what you want? A hard spanking on your wet, soapy bottom?"

"No, Daddy. I-I don't want a spanking. Not now. I want you to touch me. Please. I'll try to be good." I would say whatever he wanted to hear if only he would grant me some measure of release.

"Hold very still, little Gemma, so Daddy can inspect your privates. If you're a very good girl, I will give you special rubs to make the aching stop."

I whimpered when he pulled my cheeks even wider apart. Was he looking at my bottom hole? Or gazing at my spread pussy? I fought the impulse to press my legs closer together or sink down in the water where I might manage to quickly stroke myself to bliss before he could stop me. A quiver rushed across my ass. If I disobeyed him like that, I knew he would make me pay. He would smack my wet bottom, and I didn't think I could withstand a spanking right now. I was still a tad sore from the chastisement he'd given me yesterday.

He tapped at my bottom hole and I gasped. It took all my strength not to fall out of position. I really wanted the special rubs he'd promised. I needed to be a good girl for that to happen. If it meant holding still during a thorough inspection of my anus, I supposed I would have to endure.

My pussy quaked as he prodded my hole with

more insistence, applying delicious pressure but not quite pressing inside. Would he breach my tight entrance? Did I want him to?

Maybe.

"Have you ever taken a cock in your bottom hole before, Gemma?"

"No, never," I said with a shake of my head. "I've never taken anything in my bottom hole before. Not even a finger or a toy."

"Well, that's a shame, sweet girl, because you have the most adorable little pucker, one that begs to be claimed."

CHAPTER 24

DEREK

"DADDY WANTS TO FEEL HOW TIGHT YOUR BOTTOM hole is, baby girl. Relax and let me inside." I pressed more firmly against her pucker, until finally I breached her snug entrance and pushed into her exquisite tightness.

She made urgent keening noises in her throat and wiggled around slightly, but for the most part, she remained in position. Her obedience pleased me.

"Mm. Very tight. Now, Daddy is going to push in a bit farther, and then, as long as you keep behaving yourself, I'm going to stroke your privates, sweet girl."

A moan drifted from her lips, and she gave a brief nod. "Okay, Daddy, but please not too deep in my bottom hole. You have big fingers."

"You'll take what I decide to give you, baby girl." I thrust farther, going knuckle-deep. Before she could protest, I reached for her pussy with my other hand and immediately sought out her swollen clit.

"Oh! Oh, Daddy!" She bucked into my hand, and her bottom hole clamped down on my finger.

Fuck. I was so hard, I was sweating and practically panting as my cock strained against my jeans. I wished I'd taken my flannel shirt off before getting Gemma in the tub, but I wasn't about to withdraw my touch from her in order to lose some of my clothes.

I focused on rubbing her immense moisture overtop her clit and circling her nubbin with increasing pressure. She gasped and moaned and made the sexiest noises I'd ever heard. I kept my finger buried in her ass as I continued thrumming her clit, and it wasn't long before she cried out in the throes of a long, drawn-out release.

Soapy water sloshed onto the floor as she undulated her center against my hand, her bottom hole clamping down on my submerged finger. Perspiration trickled down my temple as I imagined what it would be like to have my cock shoved deep in her ass as she orgasmed. So fucking unbelievably tight.

Once she stopped jerking in the water and moaning, she shot me a fatigued but very satisfied look as she fought to catch her breath. I slowly withdrew my finger from her bottom and removed my hand from her pussy. After washing my hands quickly in the soapy water, I peered down at the water she'd gotten on the floor. My shirt and jeans had also gotten soaked as she'd writhed in the bath during her release.

I gave a slow, deliberate shake of my head as I

looked at her sternly. "Look at this mess you just made. Naughty, naughty little girl. I thought I told you to behave, hm?"

Her mouth dropped open with a gasp and she flushed. "Sorry, Daddy, I-I didn't mean to. Am I in trouble?" She was still in the position I'd ordered her to get into so I could clean her privates, on her hands and knees with her ass lifted in the air, her legs parted to reveal the sweetness between her thighs.

"I know it was just an accident, Gemma, but you need to remember to be more careful next time. After Daddy cleans up the floor, you're going to get a few smacks on your wet, soapy bottom. Don't move." I hurried to grab a towel and wipe up the floor, then I tossed the towel aside and gave her another stern look.

I knelt next to the tub and cupped her bottom, giving it a firm squeeze. She shuddered and made tiny whimpering sounds that went straight to my cock. Jesus. It was at that moment I realized I couldn't wait until tonight to have her as originally planned.

Before I tucked her in for a nap, I would sink my cock into her sweet little pink pussy and drive home until I spilled inside her. She would go to sleep with my seed dripping out of her to coat her inner thighs.

Wait... no. I couldn't ride her bareback. Not yet. Not this soon in our relationship. I thought of the condom in my wallet and breathed an internal sigh of relief. I was so eager to pound into her that I'd nearly forgotten about protection.

I scooped soapy water over her bottom a few

times, getting her curvy cheeks nice and wet. A spanking on a wet butt would pack an extra sting. I lifted my hand and delivered the first swat. She jolted slightly but didn't cause more water to splash onto the floor. I gave her four more quick but hard swats, just enough to redden her bottom.

"Look at this naughty baby girl who couldn't behave when Daddy gave her special rubs. You've got a bright, red butt now, Gemma." I scooped more soapy water over her bottom, loving the contrast of the white bubbles and the water cascading over her punished flesh. Between her thighs, her pussy gleamed under a fresh sheen of arousal, and her clit appeared more engorged than ever as it poked out from her nether lips.

As she gave me a bashful look, her pigtails shifted across her shoulders. "Am I all clean yet, Daddy?"

"Not yet, sweet girl. I still have to finish your privates. Hold this position for just a minute longer, please." I caressed the soapy cloth over her slick puffy nether lips, then quickly ran it through the crevice between her ass cheeks.

She shuddered and emitted tiny gasps and kept glancing over her shoulder to see what I was doing, her face beautifully flushed.

"There," I said with an air of satisfaction. "All done. You can sit back in the water." Once she'd complied, I pulled the plug and sat on the edge of the tub while it drained. "Okay, time to rinse the bubbles off you, sweetheart. Please stand up."

I helped steady her after she rose to her feet, and I

turned on the freestanding shower head that rested on the floor beside the tub, a modern fixture I was glad I'd had the foresight to install during the recent remodel of this building.

"There you go, baby girl. You're all clean now. It's time to dry you off." I reached for a towel and wrapped it around her body, then guided her to step onto the bathmat. I took my time toweling her off, paying special attention to her breasts, her red butt, and her privates.

The act of taking care of her needs called up long-forgotten desires inside me. I liked having a sweet little girl to take care of, a little girl to guide and cherish. Someone to share my life with. Gemma. In a few short days, she'd become my whole world. And God how I hoped she felt the same about me.

CHAPTER 25

GEMMA

The moment Daddy started putting my freshly washed ladybug footie pajamas on me, I stuck my lip out in a pout. I couldn't help it. I'd thought we would have grown-up fun before he put me down for a nap. I snuck a glance at his crotch. Yep, tight in the front and bulging hugely with the evidence of his desire. So why wasn't he claiming me right now?

I lowered my head, not wanting him to see my expression and ask why I was being grumpy all of a sudden. He'd just taken care of me. He'd given me a thorough bath and special rubs, and I was pretty sure I'd never climaxed so hard in my life. My legs were still trembling.

After he got my footie pajamas zipped up, he patted the drop-seat part. He tucked me into bed and pressed a lingering kiss to my forehead, but his hand soon delved between my thighs, and he gave my privates a firm squeeze that drew a moan from my throat.

"Are you taking any sort of birth control, sweetheart?" he asked, catching me off guard. "I have a condom, but I'd like to know." He cleared his throat. "I promise you I'm clean. As you know, I haven't been with anyone in years."

"I'm clean, too," I replied quickly. I'd gotten tested for everything after my nasty breakup with Kenny and I hadn't been with anyone since. Not that I felt like telling Daddy those details. "But yes, I take birth control pills. As for the condoms, are they latex?"

"Yes, why?"

"I'm allergic." I swallowed hard. "But we don't have to use one. If I'm clean, and you're clean, and I'm on birth control..." I let my voice trail off. The thought of feeling Daddy's bare cock inside me left me quivering with desire.

"Are you certain?" he asked.

"Yep, I'm certain." I also hoped this conversation was going where I thought it was.

"Do you still feel achy down here, baby girl?" he asked, pulling back to stare into my eyes.

I nodded. "Yes, Daddy. Very achy. I-I don't think I'll be able to fall asleep. Not without touching myself first. Do I have permission to touch my privates and make myself feel good?"

He released a quick breath, and I was pretty sure he uttered a curse word too, but I didn't quite catch what he said. His gaze was heated with passion, and I hoped that my faux-innocent comment about wanting to touch myself would spur him into action.

"Well, we can't have you so unsettled then, can we?" He threw the covers back and turned me on my side, making fast work of unbuttoning my drop seat. He hadn't put panties on me, so his hand caressed my bare bottom.

My pulse quickened and heat surged to my pussy. *Yes. Oh yes. Keep touching me, Daddy.*

He pressed two fingers into my core. "So wet, Gemma. You just had a bath and you're about to make another mess."

"Maybe you should do something about it, Daddy," I said, peering at him from over my shoulder.

He gave one of my pigtails a playful tug. "Maybe I should."

After guiding me to sit up, he gathered the pillows and placed them in the center of the bed. He nodded at the mound, and I suddenly understood what he wanted from me. He wanted me to place myself over the pillows, stomach down with my bottom lifted high. My heart beat faster, and a fresh tremor of desire spiraled through my body, heating me all over.

Daddy wanted to claim me from behind.

He placed a finger beneath my chin, forcing my gaze to him. "Daddy wants to help make you feel good, sweetheart. Place yourself over the pillows, baby girl, and I'll fill up your privates with my cock and pound into you from behind. Would you like that?"

All the air left my lungs in a rapid whoosh. For

several long moments, I struggled to speak. Finally, I managed to say, "Yes, Daddy, I would like that very much."

"Would you like a taste of Daddy's cock first?" He stood and started unfastening his belt and his jeans.

Oh my God. When he withdrew his huge, erect shaft, I nearly orgasmed on the spot. Daddy was huge. In fact, he was so long and thick, I feared I might struggle to accept his massive size when he finally claimed me.

"Yes," I breathed, almost a whisper. I parted my lips as he rounded the bed and crawled atop it, angling his cock toward my mouth.

"Get it nice and wet for me, sweetheart, and then I'll fill you up and give you the pounding you crave. When I finally put you down for your nap, you're going to have a sore little pussy that's dripping with my seed, aren't you?"

Damn. His dirty talk had me purring. I sucked in a quick breath as he pressed his shaft between my lips. Mm. The masculine scent of him washed over me, and I licked his cock up and down before hollowing my cheeks and taking him deeper. Too soon, he withdrew his length from my mouth, but I wasn't about to complain. Because Daddy was about to take me from behind.

"You need to get on the pillows, baby girl. Right now. You don't want another spanking, do you?"

I scrambled to obey, and once I was in position draped over the pillows, he grabbed my hips and urged my butt higher. Then he stood next to the bed as he stripped completely naked. Holy crap on a peanut butter cracker, *that body*. It was a working man's body, with defined muscles and the thickest, brawniest thighs I'd ever seen. He definitely didn't leave all the ranch work to his employees. It looked like Daddy lifted bales of hay or built log cabins for fun every day.

He climbed onto the bed and got settled behind me, and I shuddered and lifted my bottom higher. Even if he was so large that it hurt, I wanted him inside me, pounding me with deep, hard thrusts.

My breath caught in my chest as he moved my drop-seat further out of the way. He dragged the tip of his cock through my folds several times, up and down, before he started pushing inside.

Slowly. So very slowly.

"You're going to take every inch of Daddy's cock, aren't you, baby girl?"

"Yes, Daddy," I gasped out. I wanted every inch and more. I wanted all of him. His body and his heart, even his soul. I wanted to feel him coming inside me, wanted to feel his ownership. I'd never felt so possessive of a man before, but I felt possessive of Daddy. I hoped he felt the same about me.

I cried out in ecstasy when, in one quick drive, he thrust inside and filled me up completely, so fast that his scrotum slammed into my clit. He grasped my hips and I felt him tugging on the flap of my drop-seat, moving it more out of the way. I loved that he was taking me this way, as I laid over the pillows in my bed wearing my little girl jammies, my drop-seat open to expose my slick folds, his for the taking. He remained submerged in me for a while before he finally withdrew, only to slam back inside me in the next moment.

He set a fast rhythm of claiming me, his huge cock stretching me open as he thrust home repeatedly. With each rapid drive, his balls slammed heavily against my clit, priming me for another release. It hit me almost out of nowhere, and I clutched the covers and moaned as the sensation spread from my center and outward, causing my toes to curl and my knees to become weakened in the aftermath. His voice brimmed with authority. My whole body tingled and ached and hungered for more.

Daddy kept going, kept thrusting his big manhood into my center, and the sound of sticky slaps filled the room, as well as the smacking of his scrotum upon my clit. His cock swelled larger inside me, and he growled deep in his throat.

When he increased the pace of his thrusts, I fell over the edge again, crying out as another release swept over me, draining me of all energy. I fought for air as I felt the first spurt of his seed inside me. He gripped my hips harder and pounded faster, filling me up just as he'd promised.

Claiming me as his.

CHAPTER 26

DEREK

My heart swelled as I cradled Gemma in my arms. She sighed with contentment and her breath tickled my chest. I smoothed a hand over her head and absently played with one of her pigtails. God, she was perfect. And mine. All mine.

"You're my girl, Gemma," I said with my lips at her ear. "I hope you know that. You're my girl. That means you belong to me, and you're going to have a helluva time trying to get rid of me." I glanced around her room and envisioned packing up all her belongings into boxes so I could move her to the ranch. It wasn't the first time I'd thought about us living together, either.

She laced her arms around my waist and hugged me back. "I don't want to get rid of you, silly," she said with a short laugh. "I want to keep you, Daddy. I like having you as my Daddy. I feel safe and cherished with you, and I no longer feel lonely."

Lonely. This word had me reeling for a few seconds. Until I'd met her, I'd been lonely. Incredibly so. It broke my heart to know she'd been just as lonely, but thankfully, we'd found one another. Her brightness outshined all my darkness, and I hoped that my comfort and acceptance helped her feel at peace with herself. Helped her realize that she was perfect and beautiful just the way she was.

I held her for what felt like hours, though when I glanced at a clock, only thirty minutes had passed. I pressed a kiss to the crown of her head, and when she didn't shift in my embrace, I listened to her deep, steady breathing and realized she'd fallen asleep. Fallen asleep in my arms. I felt like the luckiest guy on the planet.

Instead of getting her settled under the covers, I continued holding her. I ought to have helped her clean up a little after our joining, but I could easily give her another bath after she woke up. My cock shifted at the prospect.

Two hours passed and she slept peacefully in my arms. And all the while, my heart kept swelling larger. There was no mistaking the feelings I had for her. I loved her. I'd fallen in love with her a little on the morning we'd first met, but that seed of half-love, half-infatuation had grown into something more during the past few days.

I knew in the depths of my being that I would marry this girl one day. I would marry her, and she would become my forever little girl, and I would become her forever daddy.

Finally, she started to wake up. Her eyes fluttered open, and she yawned widely. She rubbed at her face and blinked up at me, and once her eyes focused on me, she gifted me with a sweet smile.

"Good morning, Daddy. Er, good afternoon. Or is it evening?" She glanced toward the window. "I have no idea what time it is. That was the best nap ever."

"It's almost five o'clock," I replied, kissing her forehead.

She blushed as she looked at me. "Daddy, I'm sticky between my thighs. I need to go, um, clean up."

I glanced toward the master bathroom. "How about you stay here while I run you another bubble bath? I'll be right back. We'll try to make this one quick though. I was thinking we could order Chinese food and watch some movies together. And, if you're still agreeable, I will spend the night here."

Her face brightened. "That sounds perfect, Daddy! Thank you!"

I stroked my knuckles across her cheek and pressed a quick kiss to her lips. Then I hurried to the bathroom and set about preparing a bubble bath for my sweet baby girl.

❧❦❧

WE MADE LOVE SLOWLY BEFORE BEDTIME THAT night, and I took my time kissing every inch of Gemma's body. Her luscious breasts, down the flat expanse of her stomach, and lower still. I suckled on her clit until she writhed against my mouth and cried out her release.

I claimed her missionary-style, and God how I loved staring into her eyes as I thrust into her, loved watching the look of rapture that crossed her face as she came.

In the morning, we ate leftover Chinese food for breakfast and watched rain clouds roll across the sky. Finally, the skies opened, and it began pouring. The steady pounding of the rain hitting the roof made us both sleepy and eager to go back to bed.

So we did. We curled up under the covers and took a morning nap, followed by another round of slow lovemaking. The way Gemma kept looking at me, as if I were the center of her universe, stunned me to my very core. I could easily drown in those gorgeous dark eyes of hers.

Just before noon, she rushed into the bathroom for a quick shower. I'd already taken one and gotten dressed for the day (finally) and we had plans to enjoy a leisurely lunch at Kay's Diner. As I waited for her to finish getting ready, I sat at the kitchen table, drinking coffee and using my phone to catch up on business for the resort.

After replying to the final emails and text messages that had come through from my staff, I set my phone aside and got up to pour myself another cup of coffee. As I stood at the counter doing just that, Gemma's phone beeped and buzzed. She'd left it right beside the coffee maker. I glanced down and jolted at the message that flashed on the screen.

Fucking bitch. How dare you block me!

Block me all you want, burner phones are cheap.

Just like you, a cheap whore.

By the way, your mother gave me your new number.

Your parents hate you as much as I do.

Even as I saw red, I felt a bit guilty that I'd read text messages meant solely for her. I growled and watched her phone to see if any additional messages came through. Was someone threatening her?

Guess what, bitch? I have copies of the pics.

A minute passed and I continued staring at her phone in shock. My anger grew. I wanted to know who was speaking to her like this. I wanted to find out their name and address and pay them a special visit. She was my little girl and I wanted to protect her from harm.

Answer me. Answer me now, slut!

Unless you want pics of your vag on the net again, you better fucking answer.

I want my money.

Pay up or else.

I turned at the sound of footsteps. Gemma breezed into the kitchen, her hair damp from her recent shower, a smile on her face. But when her eyes met mine, her smile faded. Not that I could blame her. I probably looked like I could murder someone right now.

"What's wrong, Daddy?" Her gaze fell to her phone, and she went pale when another text came through, causing the phone to beep and buzz. I didn't look down to see what this message said, because I wanted to make sure she was okay. She swayed on her feet and I rushed to her side.

When I reached her, she made a shooing motion. "I'm okay. I'm fine. But you should go." She gripped the back of a chair, closed her eyes, and took a deep breath. "Please leave."

CHAPTER 27

GEMMA

Each time my phone beeped and buzzed, I flinched.

I felt sick to my stomach.

When I'd walked into the kitchen to find Daddy standing next to my phone wearing a murderous look, it hadn't taken long for me to realize what had happened—he'd glimpsed some angry text messages from Kenny.

While I hadn't read the messages yet, judging by the flurry of beeps that kept coming, it sounded like he was on a roll with the angry texts. He must be using another phone, a new number I hadn't blocked yet. Had he called me names? Demanded money?

My stomach dropped to the floor.

Had he mentioned the nude pics?

"Sit down, baby girl, please. You look very pale and

you're shaking. You're making me worried." His voice was gentle and calm, a stark contrast to the furious glint in his eyes. He blinked a few times and the angry look faded, and he peered at me with nothing but kindness. It broke my heart.

I shook my head. "I-I'm fine. Please go."

"Why do you want me to leave, sweetheart?"

"You know why." My voice wobbled and a few tears escaped to trickle down my cheeks. Shit. I didn't want to cry in front of him. Not when he was leaving. I'd asked him to go. Why was he still here?

He sighed and appeared suddenly regretful. "I'm sorry I read your text messages, Gemma. I didn't mean to invade your privacy like that. The first time, anyway. I was getting more coffee when I heard a beep, and I looked down and saw a message that made me very concerned. After that, I'll admit I stood there and kept reading the other texts flash on the screen." He stroked my hair and pressed a hand to my lower back, guiding me into a chair. I sank down on shaky legs and felt like sobbing, but I swallowed hard and tried to keep it together.

"I'm not mad that you read the messages. I believe you when you say you didn't mean to read them." It wasn't as though I'd caught him holding my phone and scrolling through past messages. He'd just glimpsed the new texts that had flashed on the screen.

"Then why do you want me to leave?" He knelt in front of me and clasped my hands between his. Sadness tinged his features, and I didn't understand it.

I supposed I needed to find out exactly what the messages said first.

"I..." My voice trailed off, and when another tear rolled down my face, he was quick to brush it away. "Could you please hand me my phone?"

He released a long breath, nodded, and rose to his feet. He quickly moved across the kitchen to retrieve my phone, and my hands trembled as he handed it over. Oh God. What would the texts say?

I sniffled and wiped at my face as I typed my password in and opened the message thread. It was worse than anything I could've imagined. Kenny still had the pictures of me, and he was threatening to share them.

And now Daddy knew. He knew almost everything.

Daddy. Could I even call him that anymore? I'd asked him to leave because I was so ashamed. Stupid. That was the word so many people had called me that had stung the most. Maybe I was stupid. Stupid enough to take the pics in the first place. Stupid enough to share them with Kenny. Stupid enough to believe he'd once loved me. Stupid enough to believe he'd deleted the pics after we broke up.

"Gemma, sweetheart, please talk to me. Tell me what's going on. I'm worried that someone is threatening you. Are you in some kind of trouble?"

My breaths came shallow and fast, and I gave my head a shake as the dizziness increased. I tried to take slow, long breaths and calm my mind the way my therapist had taught me. It helped. Just a little. Just enough for me to manage a few words.

"If you really want to know what this is about, I'll tell you, but it's not pretty.'" My heart sank and I berated myself for thinking I could truly start over. I should've known Kenny would somehow fuck Rocky Springs up for me too. I prayed he hadn't shared the pictures online again.

"All right," Daddy said as he pulled a chair next to me and sat down. "I want to hear everything."

I couldn't bear to look at him as he learned about my shame, so I lowered my head and stared at my hands as the full truth spilled out. I told him about the pictures and the breakup and Kenny's revenge when I refused to get back together with him. I also told him about the trial and the lawsuit I brought against my ex, as well as being awarded fifty thousand in damages.

After I finished speaking, he was silent for a long while. So quiet I started to wonder if maybe he'd zoned out and hadn't heard my story. Or maybe he was horrified by what I'd told him. But finally, he broke the silence, and his words caused fresh tears to spill from my eyes.

"Gemma, what happened to you in Westport was terrible, but it wasn't your fault, and you have nothing to be ashamed of. I'm so sorry you went through this, baby girl, and that your own parents turned their backs on you. That ex of yours is a real piece of work and I'd pay a lot of money to have a few minutes in a room alone with him. Hey," his voice was gentle, "look at me, please."

I inhaled a shuddering breath and turned to face

him. He reached for a napkin and gently blotted the tears from my cheeks. His kindness nearly broke me. Did he truly not care about what I'd done? Didn't it bother him that there might be scandalous pictures of me circulating the internet? It was a mistake that could very well follow me for the rest of my life.

"I don't want to leave, Gemma," he finally said. "I want to stay right here with you. I want to help you get through this, and whatever happens, I'll be right there with you, supporting you. Loving you."

Loving me? Had he really just said that? My mind reeled and I started to feel dizzy again but for totally different reasons. I didn't have the nerve to ask him if he truly loved me or he'd just had a slip of tongue.

"But what I did was so stupid," I said, sniffling as he wiped away more tears. "And the pictures... you haven't seen them. You don't know how obscene they are. You don't know how I posed for them. And they were live on the internet for several weeks before they were taken down. So many people saw them. He posted links to the pictures on his social media pages, so lots of people from my hometown saw them." My voice trembled. "My-my parents saw them. They said I was stupid and disgusting. Disgusting. The same thing Kenny, my ex, called me when I told him about my interest in age play. What if you start to think I'm stupid and disgusting, too?" I broke down sobbing, unable to hold my emotions at bay any longer.

Daddy lifted me in his arms and carried me to the living room. He sat down on the couch with me in his lap. He stroked my hair and held me close as he wiped at my tears using napkins he must've swiped from the kitchen. "I could never think that way about you, baby girl. I happen to care about you very much. I'm not going anywhere. Like I told you earlier in the day, you're going to have a helluva time getting rid of me. I'm your daddy and you're my baby girl."

CHAPTER 28

DEREK

I held Gemma as she sobbed, wishing I could make all her pain go away. I wanted to hop on a plane to Connecticut and beat the fuck out of her dirtbag ex, but I didn't want to leave her side. It also wouldn't help matters if I ended up in jail. Gemma needed my support and I wanted to be there for her. Somehow, we would figure out a solution.

"Little one, listen to me," I said, still stroking her hair. Her sobs were starting to subside somewhat. "What your ex is trying to do to you right now is very illegal. He's trying to extort you for money. And if he's still on probation right now, that'll be another nail in the coffin for him. The text messages on your phone seem like evidence enough to me. We need to contact the authorities and make him pay."

She sniffled and withdrew from my arms slightly

to peer up at me. "May-maybe I should just give him the money he wants. Maybe that would make this all go away. I can't go through this again. I can't have my pictures out there for everyone to see."

I pressed a napkin to her face and wiped at her tears and her runny nose. "I know you're scared, Gemma, but I don't think giving him what he wants is the solution here. Extortion is a serious offense. He could be looking at jail time, and from what you've told me, he more than deserves to be put away. Do you know for certain that he has the pictures? I would have thought that the authorities would've confiscated his computer and his phone, and any other devices he might be using to store the images."

She shrugged. "I don't know for certain that he still has the pictures. I suppose he could be lying. But yes, the authorities did confiscate his laptops, his phone, and other devices he owned. But what if he's not bluffing? He's very angry that his wages are being garnished to pay me the fifty-thousand-dollar settlement that was ordered by the judge. Oh, and he is still on probation. For a few more months, I believe."

"Well, darlin', I think the first thing we should do is contact the authorities in your hometown and let them know what's going on. Let them know your ex is trying to extort you and breaking his probation in the process."

She inhaled deeply and nodded, and I was relieved that she'd stopped crying. Her eyes were red-rimmed, and she looked sad, but there was also a glint of determination that suddenly filled her gaze. "He called me yesterday," she said, "and I let my lawyer know about it. Well, I left a message, and she hasn't called me back yet. Her brother is actually a detective in Westport, and he was very helpful during the investigation and the trial. So, if I can't reach her, maybe I could call him."

A loud ringing sounded in the kitchen, and we both turned toward the noise.

"That's my cell phone ringing." She swallowed hard. "What if it's *him* again? My ex? Kenny?"

I cupped her face and kissed her forehead. "If it's okay with you, I can go answer it. But if you want to let it go to voicemail, that's fine too. It's okay if you need more time to calm down and gather your thoughts before we take action."

"You can answer it, but could you bring my cell in here and put it on speaker phone?" She blinked fast a few times but looked more composed than she had just a minute ago.

"Sure thing, sweetheart." I kissed her forehead again and then lifted her briefly to place her on the couch. "Be right back." I dashed into the kitchen and swiped the answer button on her phone. Before I said a word, I put it on speaker as I hurried back to the living room.

"Hello," I said into the phone as I sat next to Gemma.

"Um, hello?" came a feminine voice. "This is Marla Sanchez from the Law Offices of Sanchez and Gibson. I'm looking for Gemma Wilder. I hope I don't have the wrong number."

Relief filled Gemma's eyes. "Marla, I'm so glad you called. It's me, Gemma. I'm here."

"Oh good, I'm so glad I finally reached you, Gemma. I've been trying to call you back, but this is the first time you've picked up."

"Sorry about that," Gemma said. "The reception here is spotty, but I'm glad you finally got through."

"I have some news to share with you," Marla said. "Don't panic, though! It's actually pretty good news. Good for you. Not so good for Kenny Reynolds."

I held the phone closer to Gemma and reached for her hand, giving it an encouraging squeeze. Whatever the news was, good or bad, she wouldn't have to face it alone. I would stay right here with her.

"Kenny contacted me twice," Gemma said, "and he says he still has copies of my pictures. He's threatening to share them online again if I don't give him money. He's pretty pissed off about the settlement. So, if you have good news, I'm ready to hear it. I won't lie—I'm worried right now."

"Kenny was just arrested and charged with a whole grocery list of offenses. He's definitely going to jail this time. Oh, and your pictures—he doesn't have copies of them. He confessed that he was bluffing you."

Gemma clutched her chest and released a long breath, and the tension went out of her shoulders. I hugged her to my side and kissed the top of her head, and when we pulled apart, she leaned closer to the phone and said, "That's wonderful news. What happened? Tell me everything."

"Buckle up, this is sort of a long story. After I got your message, I called my brother. He told me there was a warrant out for Kenny's arrest. Apparently, he assaulted a man at a bus stop a week ago and the whole thing was caught on camera. According to the man who was assaulted, it was a drug deal gone wrong. So, the cops were already looking for the creep.

"But Kenny was finally picked up about an hour ago. Not only did he resist arrest, but they found methamphetamine and a few thousand dollars in his jacket. And let's just say he's being very talkative. Even his lawyer can't seem to keep him from blabbing. Not only did he admit to the assault and dealing drugs, but he also admitted to trying to extort you and said he never had copies of your pictures hidden anywhere. Whew. I think that about covers it."

Thank fuck, I thought. It sounded like karma had decided to buttfuck Kenny at just the right time.

"Wow, this is a lot to process," Gemma said. "But you're right—it is good news. It's the best news. I don't think I've ever felt so relieved in my entire life. How many years do you think he'll get?"

"Well, there's a mandatory five-year sentence for first degree assault in Connecticut, and the intent-to-distribute charges alone could get him up to fifteen years. If I were betting money, I would guess he's going to get at least ten years. He's also going to get hit with a lot of fines. He's basically ruined his life."

"Thank you for calling, Ms. Sanchez," I said as I patted Gemma's thigh. She glanced over at me and cracked a smile, her eyes filled with happy tears.

"Oh?" The lawyer cleared her throat. "And to whom am I speaking right now? You didn't go cheating on me and hire another lawyer, did you, Gemma?" she said in a playful tone.

"You're speaking with Derek Bolt. He's my landlord... and my new boyfriend. Derek, meet Marla Sanchez, my lawyer and my friend."

"New boyfriend? Didn't you just arrive in Rocky Springs?"

We all shared a laugh, and I lifted Gemma and set her on my lap for the duration of the phone call. Gemma shared how we met, though kept it PG, and before the call ended she invited her lawyer friend to come out to Colorado for a visit.

After hanging up, Gemma turned to me and gave me a hesitant look. "You, um, you really don't care about what I did? You don't think less of me? You honestly don't think I'm stupid or—"

I silenced her with a kiss, cupping her face in my hands as I drank her in, this sweet baby girl who would belong to me forever. "I think you are a brave, smart, and talented woman, Gemma, and I'm thankful to have met you. No, I don't think any less of you, and I don't think you're stupid. Not at all. Please erase those worries from your mind. I care about you a lot and I hope we're together for a long, long time." *Forever.* I didn't say the word out loud, but it echoed in my head, and I meant it with all my heart.

CHAPTER 29

Two days later...

GEMMA

I didn't think I would ever get tired of going to Kay's Diner with Daddy for breakfast. Yum. Today, I'd decided to try the blueberry pancakes. I took a sip of coffee and my heart fluttered when my gaze collided with Daddy's sexy blue eyes.

He still wanted me. He hadn't judged me. Instead of rejecting me, he'd stayed by my side during one of the scariest and darkest moments of my life. I'd been so afraid Kenny was going to ruin my life again, but nothing bad had happened. Thank goodness.

"Gemma," Daddy said, and he looked suddenly nervous, "there's something I feel I should tell you.

It's about my past." He held up a hand. "Don't worry, it's nothing bad. It's about... well, I was married once."

I reached across the table and grasped his hand. "I know, Daddy, and I'm so sorry about what happened to your wife."

Confusion clouded his eyes. "How did you know?"

"On the very first day we met, after you went home, I kinda sorta Googled your name and found a few newspaper articles about the accident. Again, I'm so sorry. I saw pictures of you and Trisha together. You looked very happy and very much in love. I can't imagine what it must've been like to lose someone like that." I squirmed in my seat, feeling a tad guilty and stalkerish. Daddy was older than me by quite a few years. Maybe he didn't know it was normal behavior to look up your love interest on the net.

His brows narrowed slightly. "You Googled me? Seriously? The day we first met?"

I nodded. "Of course. I, um, hope you aren't upset. I just wanted to know more about you. I really liked you and I was curious." I shot him a comforting smile and laced my fingers through his. He squeezed my hand and sighed.

"I'm not upset you looked me up, darlin'. In fact, now that I think about it, that seems like a smart thing to do. For all you knew, I could've been a serial killer."

I grinned. "Well, you did break into my apartment."

He laughed, and I was relieved to see him happy

given the morose turn our conversation had taken. My heart ached for Daddy and the loss he'd endured. So sad and so tragic. I couldn't fathom losing him in an accident, gone in a flash. The very thought brought tears to my eyes, and I found myself blinking fast. I buried my face in my extra-large coffee mug (bless Kay) and took a long sip.

"Gemma, you're the first girl I've looked at in five years. As soon as I saw you, standing there looking so cute and innocent in your footie pajamas, I knew I wanted you as mine. I've never experienced an attraction so instant. And that first day we spent together... well, let's just say that it was healing for me. This might sound cheesy, but when I'm with you, I feel like I'm walking on a cloud."

His words made my soul rejoice. I returned his smile. "Yes, Daddy, that does sound a little cheesy," I said with a small laugh, "but it's how I feel about you too. I care about you and like having you as my Daddy."

"I like having you as my baby girl." He nodded at my plate. "Finish your breakfast, young lady, and I'll drive you out to my ranch and give you a personal tour."

I dove into my pancakes with gusto and downed the rest of my coffee.

DEREK

· · ·

I LOVED HAVING GEMMA ON THE RANCH, AND I didn't want to think about driving her back to town later. Fast as things were moving between us, though, maybe I would be able to convince her to move out here with me soon. It was only a twenty-minute drive into town, and she could still keep the brick rental property to use as her art studio. Maybe I could have a studio built for her on the ranch, too, so she could paint while she was at home whenever the mood struck her...

I smiled to myself and gave my head a shake. I was practically ready to start planning our wedding, though I didn't think I should mention that to Gemma yet. I didn't want to risk scaring her away. Not when I'd just found her. She was the missing piece of my heart, and I wasn't going to lose her.

"It's so beautiful here," she said as we walked through a meadow toward one of the hiking trails frequented by resort guests. "I also read about how you scrimped and saved so you could buy this land and build a ranch, how you spent years as a ranch hand and worked other side jobs. Then you erected one building at a time, as you could afford it, and how you started buying and fixing up buildings to turn into rentals in town. By the time you were ready to open your resort, business in town was exploding. You're highly respected in these parts."

I lifted my eyebrows at her. "You found all that information on Google?"

She giggled. "No, silly, I used Google to search for

the information, which was located on news sites and information sites about this town. You do know what Google is, don't you, old man?"

I growled at her. "Yes, I know what Google is. I own a laptop." Although I rarely cracked it open. I had people who managed the ranch's website and bookings for the resort, as well as our social media pages.

"Okay, okay, no need to get your boxers in a bunch. I was just teasing. I'm sure you know what Google is." She cast me a sidelong glance, a playful smile tugging at her lips.

"You know, back in my day, we didn't have Wi-Fi *or* Google. We had to dial into the internet with our phone lines and search the net with Yahoo or Ask Jeeves."

"Who's Jeeves?"

Now it was my turn to laugh. And also to feel old. "How old are you, Gemma? I'm a bit embarrassed that I never asked you."

"Twenty-five," she said. "Don't worry. I already know your age. I looked it up. In a couple of years, you'll be able to get a senior discount on your coffee at Kay's Diner."

I grunted. "A couple of years? The senior discount at Kay's starts at age sixty. I'm only forty-five."

She pulled me off the hiking path and into the trees, wrapping her arms around my waist and peering up at me. "I was just teasing, Daddy. You don't have to get all grumpy on me."

"I'm not being grumpy. If I were grumpy, I'd look like this." I made a funny, pretend angry face that caused her to giggle.

I leaned down to kiss her, and I swore I heard music.

EPILOGUE

THREE MONTHS LATER...

GEMMA

I WATCHED AS THE MOVERS LOADED THE LAST BOX onto the truck. Daddy stood next to me, holding my hand. We exchanged a loving glance, and he kissed me on the cheek.

Flutters rose in my stomach and warmth surged between my thighs. Damn. Even after a few months of dating, that happened almost every time he kissed me.

Yes, even just a quick peck on the cheek.

"I'm so happy you're moving to the ranch, baby girl," he said, his eyes brimming with affection. "I can't wait to wake up with you in my arms every day."

He appeared suddenly stern. "I'll also be able to keep a better eye on you. You won't be able to get away with any naughtiness, young lady."

I gave him a sassy look, and when the movers had their backs turned, I even stuck out my tongue at Daddy. His visage became even sterner and I shivered with anticipation. His body tensed and he gently turned me and pushed me in the direction of the house.

"Get inside, naughty girl, and I'll deal with you later. I just need to speak with the movers quickly."

I walked up the five stairs to the porch, my eyes on Daddy the whole time, as I took the slowest steps possible. He glanced over his shoulder just before he reached the movers and shot me another stern look that had me moving a bit faster once I reached the top of the stairs. The bell above the door jangled as I pulled it open.

Skipping into the brick house, I gazed around the first floor with an air of satisfaction. I was moving in with Daddy, but I was still keeping my art studio, though I'd closed the shop today in order to finish moving. Business was booming and I needed to be back here bright and early tomorrow morning.

I sighed with contentment as I flipped through the list of custom orders I'd placed next to my work area in the back corner of the studio. A sense of peace settled over me. I'd done it. I'd actually done it—made a fresh start in a brand-new town. Not only that, but I was truly happy. I was thriving.

The sound of a jangling bell alerted me to Daddy's presence. My heart skipped a beat as I turned to face him. Oh my. He had his arms crossed over his chest as he stood just inside the doorway, his face set in a stern expression that caused heat to gather in my center. His arms dropped to his sides, and he approached me. I pressed my thighs together, watching with bated breath as he came closer.

"I know a certain someone who is acting too big for her britches," he said.

I made a show of appearing shocked. "Oh? And who would that be, Daddy?" I glanced around the room as though searching for the person he was talking about.

He grasped my chin between his fingers, forcing me to peer directly into his eyes. "Maybe you need a spanking to remind you to behave, little Gemma." He released my chin, took one step back, and methodically rolled up his sleeves, not blinking once as his gaze remained riveted to me.

"A reminder spanking?" I gasped in feigned outrage. "That's not a thing, Daddy!"

"I assure you that reminder spankings are indeed a thing. Now, come with me, baby girl. You'll take your spanking upstairs where the neighbors or a passerby won't inadvertently glance in a window and witness you getting your bottom reddened."

I flushed. Not for the first time, the idea of receiving a punishment while others watched left me excited. Heat blossomed in my core, and I struggled for air as Daddy guided me upstairs. I could feel my panties becoming wetter and wetter as he led me into the kitchen.

We'd left the table and chairs behind since I wouldn't need them at the ranch, and Daddy grabbed one of the chairs and dragged it into the center of the room. The familiar sound that heralded an imminent spanking—the chair scraping along the floor tiles—caused a tingle to rush across my butt cheeks.

Daddy sank down on the chair and guided me to stand between his parted legs. He reached up my skirt and cupped my bottom, allowing his thumb to play with the waistband of my panties. I exhaled a shuddering breath and wondered if he would give me special rubs after my spanking.

"You've been a little mouthy this morning, haven't you, young lady?" he said in a scolding tone.

I quickly thought back on my behavior. Well, I had sniped at him a few times as we finished packing the boxes before the movers arrived. But in my defense, I hadn't had my usual two cups of coffee yet this morning. Daddy had promised to take me to Kay's Diner for a late breakfast before we headed back to the ranch.

"But Daddy," I said, stomping my foot slightly on the floor. "It's not fair. We had a lot of work to do this morning and I'm running on zero caffeine. It's not my fault if I maybe kinda sorta sniped at you a few times." My pulse quickened. He'd said this would be a reminder spanking, but now I was starting to worry he would decide I needed a punishment spanking instead.

"I respect the effort, baby girl, but you're not talking your way out of this one." His deep voice resounded with authority. "You're getting ten smacks. Ten smacks to remind you that you need to watch your attitude, baby girl." He patted his thigh. "Place yourself over my lap, Gemma. If you cooperate, I might be inclined to rub your privates and make you feel good afterward."

I took a deep breath before lowering myself over his thick, muscular thighs. He helped me get into position and wasted no time in baring my bottom, flipping my skirt up and tugging my panties down. He forced my legs wide apart and placed a steadying hand on my lower back.

"Oh!" I gasped after the first blow, which came sooner than I'd expected. Usually, Daddy kept me over his lap for a few minutes as he rubbed my bottom and scolded me before starting my spanking.

"Your privates are glistening with your arousal, little Gemma." He delivered two more firm smacks to my butt and then paused to drag one finger through my wetness.

I whimpered and bucked on his lap, aching and desperate for him to touch my clit and bring me to a release. He rewarded me with three more rapid smacks to the curve of my ass. Ouch. Daddy was spanking me hard. A sting spread across my bottom, and I wriggled over his lap, though I tried not to struggle too much. I really wanted special rubs, and I doubted Daddy would touch my privates if I misbehaved.

The final few slaps came quickly, and I heaved a sigh of relief after he reached ten. Another sigh left me when he started caressing my sore butt. Then his hand delved between my thighs, and I moaned with satisfaction as he stroked a finger over my slit, occasionally brushing over my throbbing nubbin.

"You're so adorable, little Gemma, with your bottom bright red from a spanking and your smooth pink lips gleaming with your arousal. When we get back to the ranch, Daddy's going to bend you over the bed and claim you from behind. You'll have a sore butt and a sore pussy by the time I'm through with you today."

His words sent me over the edge, and I cried out as a thunderous release swept through me, the warm pulses seizing in my center and spreading outward. I writhed over his lap, whimpering and moaning as he continued caressing my clit, wringing every last vestige of pleasure from my body.

In the aftermath of the powerful climax, I remained over his sturdy thighs, panting breathlessly. He patted my bottom and soon turned me over to sit on his lap. He wrapped his arms around me and kissed my forehead. His eyes shone with love as he stroked a hand through my hair.

"Come on, baby girl, it's time to get you home. But you'd better behave during breakfast at Kay's *and* during the drive to the ranch. If you're naughty, I won't hesitate to pull the truck over." His eyebrows lifted as he gave me his trademark playful but stern look that always made me grin.

I laced my arms around his neck and batted my eyelashes at him. "Yes, Daddy. I promise I'll be ever so good."

A DADDY FOR HANNA:

A DDlg Romance

Be a good little girl or Daddy will have to punish you...

Hanna longs for a life outside her tight-knit Amish community, and as her nineteenth birthday approaches, she finally works up the courage to leave. Her first taste of freedom comes courtesy of a ruggedly handsome English neighbor, Ben Foster, who gives her a job and a place to stay. He also gives her butterflies in her stomach and very improper thoughts that she doesn't quite understand.

After Hanna shows up at his secluded cabin and shyly asks for help, Ben finds ignoring her sweet feminine presence isn't possible when she's suddenly wearing form-fitting clothes and living under his roof. Despite his mounting desires, he tries to resist claiming her as his own. After she disobeys him during a trip to town, however, she does the unexpected—she comes to him and pleads to be punished. The intimate act of chastising her alters the nature of their relationship, and when he asks Hanna to start thinking of him as her daddy, things take a more passionate turn.

Hanna blossoms under Daddy's firm but loving guidance,

and she melts every time he calls her his baby girl. She's never experienced such tender care, and she tries to enjoy every second with Daddy because her future with him is uncertain. They're both running away from their past, and she's always planned to run far, far away. Are their paths only meant to cross for a short time, or will they discover a new road to walk together?

❧

BECOMING LITTLE LEXIE:
A Daddy Dom Romance

Daddy knows just what his little girl needs…

As Alexa's husband helps her recover from a car accident, she begins to crave his nurturing side more and more. William's firm but loving bedside manner makes her all warm and tingly inside, and she discovers she enjoys feeling like a little girl being taken care of by her daddy. But how can she tell him? What if he thinks age play is too weird?

William is stunned when his wife finally confesses what's been bothering her, but he's eager to step into the role of her daddy. More than eager, in fact. Soon he's giving her long, thorough bubble baths, reading her bedtime stories, dressing her in cute girlish dresses and drop seat pajamas, and even giving her firm spankings on her bare bottom when she's been naughty.

Alexa enjoys her special weekends with Daddy, and she tries her best to be a good girl and follow his rules. But being good isn't always easy, and she discovers time and time again there's a reason Daddy keeps her in short dresses and drop seat jammies - he wants easy access to her naughty bottom at all times.

DARK EMBRACE: THE COMPLETE SERIES

Dominant husbands, reluctant brides, and scorching hot passion…

The year is 2689, and as mankind emerges from a great societal collapse, arranged marriages and marriages of convenience have become the norm. Not only that, but wives are expected to obey their husbands in all things, or suffer firm, shameful consequences. In this deliciously naughty collection, strict but loving husbands take their blushing brides masterfully in hand, teaching them what it means to be owned, body and soul…

Features all three books in the *Dark Embrace* series:

His by Law

Saving His Runaway Bride

Papa's Little Bride

***HIS LOVING GUIDANCE:**

Three Domestic Discipline Stories*

Some husbands spank.

His Loving Guidance features three smoking hot domestic discipline stories from *USA Today* bestselling author Sue Lyndon. Corner time, firm scoldings, bare bottom spankings, and other intimate punishments await the errant wives in these deliciously naughty novellas:

Confession Time

Belonging to Ben

A Time to Heal

MARRIAGE OF CONVENIENCE

From a *USA Today* bestselling author comes this sweet and naughty 1950s romance...

When Betty is sent to her college advisor on a disciplinary matter, she doesn't expect Dr. David Bauer to scold her, make her stand in the corner, and propose marriage all within the hour. Yet that's exactly what happens, and out of desperation to escape her family's influence, the young coed finds herself saying yes to the handsome widower.

David is a strict man who has no compunction about baring his wife's bottom for a sound spanking, but he's also patient and caring. Betty feels blessed to be his wife, but she worries he views their union as nothing more than a marriage of convenience. Will he ever truly love her, and how will he react to the shameful secret she's been keeping about her past?

THE SEAL'S CAPTIVE BRIDE:
A Dark Military Romance

In the aftermath of a horrendous war, former SEAL Rick Stanford catches a pretty little thief sneaking around the settlement he's been charged to protect. Rather than see the petite brunette tried for her crimes, he protects Ally in the best way he knows how—by claiming the reluctant young woman as his wife. He's been longing for a female to call his own for quite some time, and now that he's found Ally, he'll never let her go.

The whole world has gone to hell, and Ally can't believe her only option for survival is to marry a complete stranger. She soon discovers her new husband is firm but fair. He promises to keep her safe, but he also promises to spank her bare bottom when she disobeys him. Though she wasn't the most willing of brides, Ally can't help but admire her ruggedly handsome and kind husband, and she longs for him to thoroughly claim her for the first time. But can she truly find love with the tough former SEAL who demands her obedience?

ABOUT SUE LYNDON

USA TODAY BESTSELLING AUTHOR SUE LYNDON writes naughty, heartfelt romance filled with sexy discipline, breathless surrender, and scorching hot passion. Hard alpha males, strict husbands, fierce alien warriors, and stern daddy-doms make her go weak in the knees. She's a #1 Amazon bestseller in multiple categories, including Sci-Fi Romance, Historical Romance, BDSM Erotica, and Fantasy Romance. She also writes vanilla sci-fi romance under the name Sue Mercury—but no matter the genre or pen name, her books always have a swoon-worthy happily ever after.

WWW.SUELYNDON.COM

Get FREE reads when you sign up for Sue's newsletter—and be the first to hear about freebies, sales, and new releases: https://www.suelyndon.com/newsletter-sign-up **